FLIRTY FACEOFF

(A Timberlake Titans Hockey Romance —Book Two)

FIONA GRACE

Fiona Grace

Fiona Grace is author of the LACEY DOYLE COZY MYSTERY series, comprising nine books; of the TUSCAN VINEYARD COZY MYSTERY series, comprising seven books; of the DUBIOUS WITCH COZY MYSTERY series, comprising three books; of the BEACHFRONT BAKERY COZY MYSTERY series, comprising six books; of the CATS AND DOGS COZY MYSTERY series, comprising nine books; of the ELIZA MONTAGU COZY MYSTERY series, comprising nine books (and counting); of the ENDLESS HARBOR ROMANTIC COMEDY series, comprising nine books (and counting); of the INN AT DUNE ISLAND ROMANTIC COMEDY series, comprising seven books (and counting); of the INN BY THE SEA ROMANTIC COMEDY series, comprising five books (and counting); of the ALICE BLOOM COZY MYSTERY series, comprising five (and counting); of the MAID AND THE MANSION COZY MYSTERY series, comprising five books (and counting); of the MAGNOLIA BAY COZY MYSTERY series, comprising five books (and counting); and of the TIMBERLAKE TITANS HOCKEY ROMANCE series, comprising five books (and counting).

Fiona would love to hear from you, so please visit www.fionagraceauthor.com to receive free ebooks, hear the latest news, and stay in touch.

ISBN: 979-8-89482-509-0

BOOKS BY FIONA GRACE

MAGNOLIA BAY COZY MYSTERY
THE TAINTED TAFFY (Book #1)
A MASKED MURDER (Book #2)
A CAFE CONFESSION (Book #3)
THE FROZEN FIND (Book #4)
A CURIOUS CURSE (Book #5)

TIMBERLAKE TITANS HOCKEY ROMANCE
RINKSIDE ROMANCE (Book #1)
FLIRTY FACEOFF (Book #2)
MELTING THE ICE (Book #3)
THE PUCK STOPS HERE (Book #4)
GLOVES DROP, LOVE BLOOMS (Book #5)

ALICE BLOOM COZY MYSTERY
MURDER IN THE MARIGOLDS (Book #1)
RUIN IN THE ROSES (Book #2)
DECEIT IN THE DAFFODILS (Book #3)
SCANDAL IN THE SAFFRON (Book #4)
CATASTROPHE IN THE CARNATIONS (Book #5)

THE MAID AND THE MANSION COZY MYSTERY
A MYSTERIOUS MURDER (Book #1)
A SCANDALOUS DEATH (Book #2)
A MISSING GUEST (Book #3)
AN UNSOLVABLE CRIME (Book #4)
AN IMPOSSIBLE HEIST (Book #5)

INN BY THE SEA ROMANTIC COMEDY
A NEW LOVE (Book #1)
A NEW CHANCE (Book #2)
A NEW HOME (Book #3)
A NEW LIFE (Book #4)
A NEW ME (Book #5)

THE INN AT DUNE ISLAND ROMANTIC COMEDY

A CHANCE LOVE (Book #1)
A CHANCE FALL (Book #2)
A CHANCE ROMANCE (Book #3)
A CHANCE CHRISTMAS (Book #4)
A CHANCE ENGAGEMENT (Book #5)
A CHANCE DREAM (Book #6)
A CHANCE WEDDING (Book #7)

ENDLESS HARBOR ROMANTIC COMEDY
ALWAYS, WITH YOU (Book #1)
ALWAYS, FOREVER (Book #2)
ALWAYS, PLUS ONE (Book #3)
ALWAYS, TOGETHER (Book #4)
ALWAYS, LIKE THIS (Book #5)
ALWAYS, FATED (Book #6)
ALWAYS, FOR LOVE (Book #7)
ALWAYS, JUST US (Book #8)
ALWAYS, IN LOVE (Book #9)

ELIZA MONTAGU COZY MYSTERY
MURDER AT THE HEDGEROW (Book #1)
A DALLOP OF DEATH (Book #2)
CALAMITY AT THE BALL (Book #3)
A SPEAKEASY DEMISE (Book #4)
A FLAPPER FATALITY (Book #5)
BUMPED BY A DAME (Book #6)
A DOLL'S DEBACLE (Book #7)
A FELLA'S RUIN (Book #8)
A GAL'S OFFING (Book #9)

LACEY DOYLE COZY MYSTERY
MURDER IN THE MANOR (Book#1)
DEATH AND A DOG (Book #2)
CRIME IN THE CAFE (Book #3)
VEXED ON A VISIT (Book #4)
KILLED WITH A KISS (Book #5)
PERISHED BY A PAINTING (Book #6)
SILENCED BY A SPELL (Book #7)
FRAMED BY A FORGERY (Book #8)
CATASTROPHE IN A CLOISTER (Book #9)

TUSCAN VINEYARD COZY MYSTERY
AGED FOR MURDER (Book #1)
AGED FOR DEATH (Book #2)
AGED FOR MAYHEM (Book #3)
AGED FOR SEDUCTION (Book #4)
AGED FOR VENGEANCE (Book #5)
AGED FOR ACRIMONY (Book #6)
AGED FOR MALICE (Book #7)

DUBIOUS WITCH COZY MYSTERY
SKEPTIC IN SALEM: AN EPISODE OF MURDER (Book #1)
SKEPTIC IN SALEM: AN EPISODE OF CRIME (Book #2)
SKEPTIC IN SALEM: AN EPISODE OF DEATH (Book #3)

BEACHFRONT BAKERY COZY MYSTERY
BEACHFRONT BAKERY: A KILLER CUPCAKE (Book #1)
BEACHFRONT BAKERY: A MURDEROUS MACARON (Book #2)
BEACHFRONT BAKERY: A PERILOUS CAKE POP (Book #3)
BEACHFRONT BAKERY: A DEADLY DANISH (Book #4)
BEACHFRONT BAKERY: A TREACHEROUS TART (Book #5)
BEACHFRONT BAKERY: A CALAMITOUS COOKIE (Book #6)

CATS AND DOGS COZY MYSTERY
A VILLA IN SICILY: OLIVE OIL AND MURDER (Book #1)
A VILLA IN SICILY: FIGS AND A CADAVER (Book #2)
A VILLA IN SICILY: VINO AND DEATH (Book #3)
A VILLA IN SICILY: CAPERS AND CALAMITY (Book #4)
A VILLA IN SICILY: ORANGE GROVES AND VENGEANCE (Book #5)
A VILLA IN SICILY: CANNOLI AND A CASUALTY (Book #6)

CHAPTER ONE

Despite the chill in the morning air, I'm sweating buckets as I step out of my car, the grandiose facade of the Timberlake Titans' training facility looming before me. Tying my auburn hair up into a no-nonsense ponytail, I take a deep breath as I grab my backpack, trying to steady the flutter of nerves in my stomach. Today marks the beginning of something monumental—my first day as the team physiotherapist.

Every step toward the entrance feels like wading through deep waters, my anticipation building with each stride. I'm no stranger to pressure, having chased the rush of competition on the track in high school and college, but this is different. Here, it's not just about running; it's about carving a place for myself in a world where every second counts, not just on the clock, but in recovery and resilience.

I pull open the heavy glass door, the sounds of clinking weights from the gym greeting me like an intimidating symphony. The place is a class act, truly state-of-the-art, not just with a rink but with a massive gym, racquetball courts, a three-story rock-climbing wall in the lobby, you name it—it's practically a shrine to all kinds of fitness. My one-season contract feels suddenly tangible in my pocket, a paper testament to the opportunity and challenge that lie ahead. A quick glance around confirms what I already know—I need to make the best impression, prove that I am more than capable of handling the physical strains and sprains of these titans of ice hockey. Otherwise, I'm history.

With my phone in hand, I thumb a message to my best friend, Naomi, the one person who knows the weight of this moment as much as I do: *I'm here! Wish me luck!*

The text bubble floats away, carrying with it a silent plea for the kind of luck that can withstand the test of muscle and sinew.

And of course, gorgeous, athletic guys. My Achilles' heel. I've had far too many encounters with cute jocks that ended in sorrow, because all they wanted was a little fun instead of a commitment. Right now, I don't need a man. I need a job. *This* job, which fell like a dream into my lap after I'd sent out round after round of applications. A season-long contract with the Timberlake Titans. I couldn't have asked for better.

Well, except for maybe a permanent contract.

Good luck! But you don't need it! You got this! she responds immediately as I head for the back of the facility. I was only here once before, for my interview, and back then, it seemed a lot less intimidating. The sweat is pouring down my ribcage now.

As I tuck my phone back into my bag, I push through the double doors leading to the locker room. The scent of sweat and determination fills the air, mingling with the sound of banter and the jostle of bodies. They are giants in their own right—towering figures clad in pads and jerseys, exuding an effortless camaraderie that I admire yet find daunting.

Ignoring the stares and bare, muscled bodies of the men, I navigate the maze of lockers, each emblazoned with a name and number, symbols of identity and pride. My assigned workspace is a haven amidst the chaos, a small corner equipped with medical supplies and a treatment table. The sight of it sparks a flicker of confidence within me. This is my domain, where I will wield tape and therapy like weaponry against injury. I will be victorious.

Trying to blend into the background, I check my bag. It's full of bandages, cold packs, and massage oils. The players continue to flow around me, rivers of testosterone and ambition, paying no attention to the newcomer in their midst. I remind myself that I belong here, that my DPT degree, three years of expertise at a PT clinic in downtown Newport, and dedication to sports medicine have earned me this spot. I will not be intimidated by their size or their sport; I am Lara Bennett, and I've conquered greater adversaries than first-day jitters.

I take a moment to look up, absorbing the scene. These athletes are now my responsibility, and I'm determined to rise to the occasion. With each piece of equipment I set in its rightful place, I feel my resolve hardening. This is where I start proving myself, where I turn anticipation into action. And I'm ready.

My fingers pause on the strap of a neoprene brace when a voice, sharp as skates on ice, slices through the buzz of the locker room. I glance up and there's the legendary Pat Lawson, the toughest screw that ever did a turn in hockey. She strides in, clipboard in hand, commanding the space like a general before battle. Her voice doesn't just carry; it charges, ricocheting off the walls and into the attentive ears of every player present. She points, she gestures, her body language exuding an authority that brooks no argument.

"Discipline is not a suggestion, gentlemen, it's the spine of this team!" Her words are stern, echoing her reputation as a bastion of tradition in the ever-evolving world of hockey. Even from this distance, I can see the fire in her eyes, the set of her jaw—unwavering, unyielding. It's clear she's a woman who has fought tooth and nail for respect in this arena, a fortress amidst these titans of timber and ice.

I've read about Pat Lawson, but seeing her in the flesh is a whole other degree of intimidation. She's new to the Titans this season, but she's led three teams to championships. Nothing quite prepared me for the real-life force of nature standing mere yards away. I'm under no illusions; winning her over will be a challenge akin to breaking through ice with bare hands. But I didn't come here to back down. Like Pat, I too know about fighting uphill battles, about overcoming odds that seem insurmountable.

"Dr. Bennett?" The sudden address snaps my attention away from the coach.

Dr. Andrews looms near me, his gaze not so much examining as it is dissecting. I've only met him once before, in passing, during my interview. He's the doctor whose shoes I'm going to be filling, as he steps back into a more supervisory role. With his beady eyes and his sneer, he reminds me of a weasel. I shake his hand. "Nice to see you again, Doctor."

"Yes. Likewise. I see you've found our little corner of the world." He runs an eye over my things.

"Yes, if that's okay. I figured I should get ready to jump in right away…"

He nods. "Yes, well, there are some things you should be aware of, with the team and how Coach Lawson runs things. She's very particular. I've seen your resume. Impressive schools, but to be honest, we're concerned about your… unconventional techniques." His tone drips with disdain, heavy enough to drown out any trace of welcome.

"Dr. Andrews," I begin, steady despite the way my heart thumps against my ribs, "my methods may be newer to the field, but they're backed by solid research and successful case studies." My words are firm, rooted in hours of study and practice, each sentence a testament to my qualifications. "I believe in integrating traditional therapy with innovative approaches to optimize recovery times and prevent future injuries."

He raises one eyebrow, skepticism etched into the lines on his forehead. "You'll find that Coach Lawson values experience and proven techniques here. This isn't a place for experimentation. You might have a hard time convincing her. Just FYI."

"Respectfully," I counter, meeting his gaze without flinching, "every established method was once a new idea. I'm here to bring the best care to the team, using all tools at my disposal."

I am the sum of my trials, the embodiment of adaptation and resilience. I won't let this guy's doubt undermine my confidence or cloud my purpose. This is no longer Dr. Andrews's domain. It's mine. Dr. Lara Bennett does not shrink back; she rises, always.

I try to remind myself of that as Dr. Andrews leaves. I take a deep breath as I listen to the cacophony of clanging weights and grunts that fill the Timberlake Titans' training facility. This is the pulse of the team, the heartbeat where every sinew and muscle is primed for battle on the ice.

"Hey, Bennett, right?" Another voice slices through the noise, a player with a tape-wrapped wrist extended toward me. "Our new PT?"

"Correct," I answer, motioning him to sit. "And you are?"

"Ethan." He hands me his wrist. "I'd offer to shake but that'll probably hurt too much."

I smile. Right. Ethan Clarke, the captain. It's so hard to put names to all these muscle-bound men. "What happened here?"

"Twisted it during drills last week. It's been nagging." His brow furrows as he watches me remove the tape and palpate his wrist, my touch light but sure.

"Looks like a mild sprain. We'll need to reduce inflammation and support it," I explain, reaching for a compression wrap. My hands work deftly, a dance they've mastered over countless injuries—each one a story, a hurdle to overcome, much like my own.

As I secure the bandage, snippets of conversation filter to my ears from the locker area. Mentions of a night out, a clash about missed passes during practice, the usual ebb and flow of camaraderie and competition that defines team dynamics. But there's an edge to their voices, a tension that speaks of more than just game strategies or social plans. It's this undercurrent I know I'll need to navigate, a riptide beneath the surface bravado.

"Thanks," a grateful Ethan says, flexing his wrist. "Feels better already."

"Keep it wrapped during activities and ice it tonight," I advise, all the while my mind picking apart the threads of dialogue around me. Understanding these players isn't just about treating their injuries; it's about treating them—knowing their fears, their motivations, their breaking points.

"Will do, Doc." He grins, pushing up from the table with a nod of thanks before rejoining the others.

I wipe down the table, preparing for the next player, when laughter erupts from the corner of the room. A joke has been shared, one of those inside quips that bond a team, yet can set someone apart if not in the loop. I'm an outsider here, a fact made more apparent with each chuckle that doesn't include me.

"New physio, huh?" Yet another voice approaches, belonging to a forward with a reputation for speed and a hamstring that's seen better days.

"Yep, I'm Lara," I say, gesturing to the table. "Let's take a look at that leg."

"Hope you've got some magic hands. We need all the help we can get this season," he says, the lightheartedness in his tone belying the pressure they're all undoubtedly feeling.

"Magic might be overstating it, but I'll do my best," I reply, keeping my tone professional yet friendly as I assess his muscle strain.

The chatter continues around me, the push and pull of egos and expectations. I listen, I learn, and above all, I work. Each assessment, each treatment, is another step toward earning my place here among the Titans.

I'm aligning a player's knee brace when the air shifts, signaling an authority that commands instant attention. I straighten up in time to see Coach Lawson heading my way, her gaze as sharp as the skates gliding across ice during a power play.

"Dr. Bennett," she greets me, her voice firm, leaving no room for casual banter. "I've heard about your 'innovative techniques' from Dr. Andrews. I trust you understand that in this league, we value tradition and discipline above all. That's why I hated for Andrews to move away from treating our players."

Her words hang between us like a challenge. I meet her steady gaze, my resolve unfaltering. "I respect the traditions of hockey," I begin, keenly aware of the eyes now fixated on our exchange. "But I also believe that integrating modern sports therapy can prevent injuries and speed up recovery times. It's about enhancing performance without sacrificing the integrity of the sport."

Pat's eyebrow arches slightly, a silent acknowledgment of my conviction, yet her stance remains unyielding. "This game isn't played in therapy rooms. It's fought on the ice, where discipline has kept this team strong." She pauses, her eyes scanning the room, filled with her players—her responsibility. "Don't let your methods undermine that."

"Of course not," I reply, my voice steady despite the flutter of anxiety in my chest. "My goal is to complement the discipline with a fresh perspective that could benefit the team."

"Could," she echoes thoughtfully, her doubt piercing. "We'll see if results follow your confidence."

She moves to leave, then turns, assessing me.

"You're pretty."

I stare at her, not sure whether it's a compliment. The way she says it, it sounds like a negative. "Thank you?"

She shakes her head as her eyes catch on my bare ring finger. "One thing I do not approve of is canoodling with the players. You're here to work. You understand?"

I frown. I guess that's what she thinks of me. I'm a pretty young girl who just took this job in order to *canoodle*, whatever that is. "Of course. I came here to work, Coach. To prove myself an asset to the team."

She gives a tight nod. With that, she turns away, leaving a trail of contemplation in her wake. Her words echo in my mind—a litany of challenges I'll have to face head-on. My qualifications are solid; my methods, though unconventional, have proved their worth time and again. But will that be enough here, amidst the Titans and their old-guard leader?

The locker room buzz resumes, but the undercurrent of Pat's doubt in my abilities lingers, clinging to my thoughts like frost to winter branches. Can I truly bridge the gap between innovation and tradition? The question looms over me, daunting in its uncertainty.

As I pack up my supplies, feeling the weight of the day's encounters, I suddenly catch sight of him. He's leaning against the doorway, his hair catching the light, his eyes focused intently on me. His smile is warm, disarming, and for a moment, I forget the icy grip of doubt. Even from across the room, I can imagine the warmth of his hand, calloused from years of playing, yet gentle and reassuring at the same time. His body language exudes confidence and ease.

“Hey,” he calls out softly, just as I’m about to exit. “You’ll do great.”

The words, simple and sincere, cut through the noise, striking a chord within me. And then it happens—that inexplicable pull in the pit of my stomach, the kind that defies logic or reason. He’s gorgeous, undeniably so, with a presence that’s both calming and exhilarating. Is this what they call love at first sight?

A flush of warmth spreads across my cheeks, and I realize I’m swooning—literally swooning—over a player I’ve just met. This isn’t me; I’m the professional, the one who keeps her head in the game. But his encouragement feels genuine, a beacon amidst all those people who don’t believe I have what it takes to succeed in this business.

“Thanks,” I manage to say, hoping my voice doesn’t betray the sudden race of my heart.

As I step into the corridor, his words linger with me—the promise of support, the hint of something more. But I can’t afford distractions, not when my career hinges on proving myself this season. I square my shoulders, determined to focus on my work, to earn my place, to extend my contract.

Yet, as I leave the Titans’ territory behind, I can’t shake the feeling that this encounter, however brief, may have just complicated everything.

CHAPTER TWO

My second day at the job is just as busy as my first. I knew that working for a hockey team would keep me on my toes, and I knew the Titans were hardcore, but I didn't know they were *this* hardcore. Every one of them comes off the ice looking like they've been through a war.

And this is just practice? What am I in for during an actual game?

No wonder Dr. Andrews is moving into a supervisory role. It'll probably be easier. I'm half his age, and by the end of the first day, I was absolutely exhausted. Last night, I fell asleep in front of the TV, fully clothed, a bowl of ramen noodles in my lap, not ten minutes after I stepped through my new apartment's door.

Now, my back aches as I kneel beside the bench, my hands expertly wrapped around a player's ankle, securing it with a practiced ease. This is the nature of the business, but I'm not used to practically caring for an entire minor-league hockey team on my own. The locker room buzzes with adrenaline, a cacophony of slamming lockers and boisterous chatter as players shed their armor of sweat-soaked jerseys and pads. Each movement is methodical, each strip of tape smoothly applied—a ritual as familiar to me as the sprinter's track once was.

"Keep off it for a couple of days, ice regularly," I instruct, my voice steady despite the undercurrent of tension that prickles the air like static. It's palpable, the sort of electricity that precedes a storm, and it's not just the usual high spirits of a team riding the wave of victory.

My attention shifts, drawn by the sharp rise in volume, and I straighten up, tucking a stray strand of hair behind my ear. Two players stand toe-to-toe, their faces flushed, voices raised in an argument that seems to have snatched the focus from everyone else. Both men are bare-chested, wearing nothing but their hockey shorts. It's a meeting of sweaty muscles, mesmerizing eye-candy, so as much as I try to tear my gaze away, I can't. My eyes flick between them, noting the clenching jaws and the way their teammates give them a wide berth, no one eager to step into the line of fire.

"Wild" Wes Carter. His reputation precedes him. He's the one the reporters love to gossip about, and with good reason. Not only is he dangerously sexy, with his longish dark hair, hazel eyes, a reckless smirk, and loads of untamed energy, but he also has the fiery attitude to match. He throws his hands up dramatically, the tattoos on his packed biceps dancing with the motion. There's something wildly captivating about him, even now, in the heat of conflict. He's a flame, and like a moth, I'm helplessly drawn in, though I know the danger that comes with getting too close.

Tyler "T-Rex" Rexall is another wild card. Standing like an immovable mountain of muscle, he breathes hard, his brow furrowed in frustration. Apparently, he was worse last year, but now he has a girlfriend who keeps him in line. But he looks about ready to burst with fury over something Wes did. Their spat is more than just a disagreement; it's a collision of two forces—Wes's wild charm against T-Rex's imposing stability.

"Easy, guys," someone murmurs, a futile attempt at calm that goes ignored.

The tension escalates, a tangible increase in the locker room's temperature, and I find myself caught in the crossfire of their heated words. Something about a play—Wes hogging the puck during a play. It's not just their tempers flaring; there's something deeper, a fracture within the team that threatens to split open with every barbed word exchanged.

And there I am, stuck in the middle, my professional concern for the team's unity mingling with a dangerous fascination for the man whose very presence spells trouble. Wes's beautiful looks are an unwelcome distraction, stirring a warmth within me that has no place in the cool, clinical confines of my work.

"Guys, come on," I hear myself say, but the words are lost, swallowed by the roar of egos and the thudding of my own traitorous heart.

The air crackles with hostility, the spat between Wes and T-Rex escalating beyond a mere exchange of words. "You don't take anything seriously, do you, Carter?" T-Rex's voice booms, filling the room with its deep timbre.

"Maybe you should lighten up, big guy," Wes snaps back, his tone deceptively light but his eyes sparking with defiance. "You were actually fun once. Remember? Before you got hitched to your old ball and chain?"

Their body language speaks volumes, more so than their words. Wes, lean and taunting, is all lithe movement, a coiled spring ready to release. T-Rex stands like a towering oak, arms crossed over his chest, an impenetrable fortress of muscle and sinew. It's a dance of fire and stone, each trying to outdo the other, neither willing to back down.

I stay on the periphery, my hands momentarily still on the ankle I'm taping, my gaze flicking from one to the other. This isn't just about pride; there's a power struggle here, something that could unravel the fragile thread holding this team together.

"Enough!" The authority in my voice surprises even me as I step forward, driven by an instinct to heal more than just physical wounds. "What's this really about?"

They both turn to me, expressions shifting. T-Rex's face softens slightly, acknowledging my presence, while Wes gives me a look that's part challenge, part amusement—like he's sizing me up, wondering if I'll be another conquest or a worthy opponent.

"Team dynamics," T-Rex grumbles, his gaze moving back to Wes. "Some of us are trying to keep things more professional. But this clown thinks he can play all our positions by himself."

"Damn straight." Wes chuckles, a sound that ripples through the tension. "And some of us know how to win without sucking the joy out of the game."

"Is this about that mid-ice collision?" I ask, my therapist's mind piecing together the puzzle. "Because if it is, then let's address it constructively. You could've worked together a little better. You weren't a team."

"See, she gets it. Give the puck to the guy who can score," Wes says, gesturing toward me. "Why can't you?"

"Because it's not just about one play," T-Rex counters, his jaw set. "It's about attitude, commitment—"

"Alright, let's take a breath," I interrupt, feeling the weight of their stares, the heat of the argument. "Let's talk this through, find a middle ground. For the team."

For a moment, there's silence, charged and heavy, and I wonder if I've stepped too far into the fray. But I stand my ground, ready to mediate, to mend what's broken. After all, isn't that what I'm here for?

Wes leans back against a row of lockers, a lazy grin spreading across his face as he locks eyes with me. There's an undeniable magnetism about him, despite the chaos he stirs up. His laughter from moments ago still hangs in the air, a melody that seems to dance around the tension.

"Look at it this way, sweetheart," Wes addresses me, his voice smooth and self-assured. "A little fire on the team keeps things interesting. You don't want us getting complacent, do you?" He cocks an eyebrow, a silent challenge woven into his words.

I'm momentarily caught off guard by the spark in his eyes, so similar to mine yet entirely different—alive with mischief and defiance. It's hard not to be drawn to that kind of energy, even when you know it's the kind that burns.

"Interesting isn't quite the word I'd use," I retort, trying to keep my tone professional. "And there's a difference between complacency and self-destruction."

"Self-destruction?" T-Rex snorts, throwing an accusatory look at Wes. "You mean like ignoring play calls for personal glory?"

"Personal glory wins games," Wes shoots back, but there's a flicker of something else in his gaze—a hint of vulnerability that he quickly masks.

It's then I realize there's more at stake here than just bruised egos and frayed tempers. The pressure to perform, to live up to expectations—it's something I understand all too well. And maybe Wes feels that pressure more than anyone, hiding behind his reckless bravado.

"It's always the spotlight for you, right, Wild? You can't just be center. You have to be center of attention," T-Rex bites out.

"Winning is a team effort," I say, trying to steer them back to common ground. "It's about trust, cooperation. You both know that."

"Trust goes both ways," Wes counters, and there's a sincerity in his voice that tugs at me, peeling away the layers of my frustration. "If T-Rex would take the stick out of—"

"Fine," I cut in, feeling the heat rise in my cheeks. It's a dangerous warmth, one that comes from standing too close to the flame. I'm acutely aware of Wes's proximity, the way his presence seems to pull at me like gravity.

"Nothing about this guy is fine," T-Rex snarls.

"Maybe we should all take five," I suggest, hoping my voice doesn't betray the turmoil inside. There's an attraction to Wes, no doubt about it, but it's tangled up with concern. Concern that if left unchecked, his impulsive nature could hurt the team—or worse, himself.

Wes turns to me, tilting his head and sizing me up as if noticing me for the first time. As if I haven't been sitting in their locker room for the past two days. "And just who are you, sweetheart?"

"I'm your doctor. Your new PT," I say, sticking my chin out, even though my words sound weak, even to me.

He lets out a little chuckle, as if he doesn't believe it.

I narrow my eyes. What a jerk.

"Okay. Sure thing, *Doc*," Wes says with a condescending lilt in his voice, pushing off from the lockers with a fluid grace that belies the tension of moments before.

I put my hands on my hips. "I *am* your PT, and if you want to be able to walk after our next session, you'd better remember that."

His eyes widen for a moment. I've thrown him off balance, thank god. But he quickly recovers. He throws me a wink, confident and disarming, before walking away.

My heart thumps erratically as I watch him, a mix of relief and disappointment churning within. He sheds the rest of his hockey uniform, leaving me staring agog at his muscled, naked backside as he struts into the showers. Before he disappears, he waves a hand at me without turning around, because he obviously just knows I'm gawking.

I wish I could unsee that. But I know I never will. I'll probably still be seeing it in my dreams tonight.

All thought has left my brain as I turn back to T-Rex. What was I talking about? Oh, right. I was ready to mend another fracture in the team's unity. But as I meet his expectant gaze, my mind can't help but wander back to Wes, to the enigma wrapped in a smile and a dare.

"Let's figure this out," I say to T-Rex, but my resolve wavers. Because part of me knows that "Wild" Wes Carter isn't just a problem to solve—he's a riddle that could unravel me completely.

CHAPTER THREE

The clock ticks past seven, and the buzz of fluorescent lights mixes with the hum of my thoughts as I thumb through the last of the patient files. It's late; the facility is quiet except for the distant sound of a Zamboni smoothing ice in the rink. I stretch, feeling the pull in muscles that haven't forgotten their sprinter's training, even if it's been years since they've hit a track.

"Almost done," I murmur to myself, sealing the folder shut with a sense of finality. I'm alone in the therapy room, surrounded by the scent of antiseptic and liniment, relics of a day spent tending to athletes' strains and sprains. Most would have headed home by now, but something about the solitude of an empty facility always brings me a strange sense of peace.

I stand, giving a final stretch, and decide on a quick walk before locking up. As I pass by the rink's viewing window, the scraping of skates against ice catches my attention.

Jamie Duncan, number 12 on his jersey and the weight of dedication on his shoulders, is out there doing drills long after the rest of the team has called it a day. It's just him on one end of the ice, the Zamboni on the other.

He's the gorgeous player I saw on the first day, the only one who gave me some encouragement. I haven't spoken to him since then, but he always has a warm smile for me. Where Wes's presence is like a thorn in my side, Jamie's is like a soothing balm. From my vantage point behind the glass, I watch him weave between cones with a precision that speaks of innate talent honed by relentless practice. He's a blur of motion, each stride pushing the limits of speed and grace on the slick surface. The arena's cold seeps through the window, but I can't tear my eyes away from the display of sheer athleticism.

"Hey, Jamie!" I call out, stepping through the door onto the frosty rinkside. "Looking good!"

I don't expect him to, but he glides over, a smile breaking across his face that softens the hard lines of exertion. His hair is darker, damp with sweat, sticking to his forehead, and those eyes of his hold a spark that's more alive than the tired fluorescents above.

"Still working hard, I see," I say, leaning against the boards.

"Always," he replies, catching his breath. "Gotta keep sharp. But Bud over there wants me to call it a day. He might run me over if I stay out much longer."

I laugh as he waves at the Zamboni driver. "You were great out there. I mean, you're always good, but tonight…" My words trail off as I think of all the times I pushed my own body beyond its limits, chasing dreams that felt as close as the ice beneath his skates.

"Thanks, Lara." He leans on his stick, looking every bit the handsome athlete without really trying. "It is Lara, right? Or should I call you Doctor?"

"Lara is fine," I say, a playful skepticism in my voice, though a part of me thrills at the acknowledgment.

"Cool." He straightens up, a seriousness replacing the easygoing charm. "Actually, I was about to grab a drink at Rusty's to wind down. You want to join me?"

Surprise flutters in my chest, unexpected and not entirely unwelcome. "Sure," I answer, a smile finding its way to my lips. "I'd like that."

"Great," he says, his grin infectious. "Let me hit the showers and I'll meet you out front in fifteen?"

I nod and walk toward the exit, the promise of warm conversation over drinks casting a glow on the evening that no overhead light could ever match.

***

The clink of glasses and the murmur of conversations envelop us as we settle into a booth at the corner of Rusty's, a little hole in the wall around the corner from the training facility. Jamie's posture, usually so upright on the ice, now carries a hint of weariness as he leans back against the leather seat. The dim lighting throws shadows across his face, giving him an air of vulnerability I haven't seen before.

"Thanks for coming out with me," he says, his voice lower than the buzz around us. He takes a sip from the glass in front of him, then sets it down, running a hand through his hair, which is still damp from the shower.

“Of course,” I reply, my fingers curling around my own drink, the cool condensation grounding me in the moment. “It’s nice to get away from the rink sometimes.”

He nods, a half-smile flickering across his lips before fading. There’s a hesitation, a breath held in, then released. “You know, my brother used to play hockey too,” he starts, his gaze fixed on the worn tabletop. “He was good—really good.”

I lean forward, drawn into his narrative by the somber tone in his voice. “Was?”

Jamie’s eyes lift to meet mine, a stormy blue. “Yeah.” His jaw tightens. “He got injured—badly—a few years back. Never played again.”

My heart contracts at the pain lacing his words.

“I’m sorry to hear that,” I say gently. My mind races back to the days of therapy rooms, of striving to heal wounds deeper than flesh and bone.

“Thanks.” He swallows hard, the lines of his face etched with the weight of memories. “It’s just… when it happened, I felt this guilt, you know? Like why should I keep playing when he couldn’t?”

“Survivor’s guilt,” I murmur, understanding without needing further explanation. “I know how that is. I was supposed to be a great runner. Almost qualified for the Olympics. Then I had a career-ending injury, and it all came crashing down. But after spending time with the physical therapist, I realized that was something I wanted to do.”

“Even more than running?”

I nod.

“I don’t know if I could love anything more than hockey,” he says, appreciation softening the furrow between his brows. “But Benny’s injury made me push harder, work longer. I want to succeed, not just for myself, but for him too. To make our family proud.”

Listening to Jamie, I see the reflection of my own past ambitions, the drive that once fueled my every step on the track. I understand the determination that pushes him to excel, the dedication that keeps his skates slicing through the ice long after others have left.

“Making them proud by being the best version of yourself,” I offer, my voice steady despite the emotions swirling within. “That’s all anyone can ask for, Jamie. Your brother, I’m sure he’s proud of you already.”

A silence settles over us, comfortable in its depth as we both take a moment, lost in thoughts of what could have been and what still might be. We are two athletes connected by shared experiences, by the thin line between triumph and loss that we tread each day.

"Thanks, Lara," he finally says, lifting his glass toward me in a quiet toast. "Means a lot, hearing that from someone who understands."

"So...you love hockey more than anything," I venture, curious. "Does that mean you've never been in a serious relationship?"

He shakes his head. "I've always been too busy on the ice, I guess. I never really had time to date. You?"

"Same, with PT." I smile. "The longest I ever dated anyone was a couple months, and that was in high school. Guess we're just too focused on our careers, huh?"

He nods. "Yeah. But I'm open to it now. You know?"

I do know. I've thought about getting serious with a guy, but most of the guys I've met have been cute jocks that never wanted more than a fling. Not exactly commitment-minded. I'm twenty-six now, and a lot of my friends have serious boyfriends and are getting engaged. I really don't know where they find these guys. I expected I wouldn't find it here, with more jocks who eat, sleep, and live hockey.

So Jamie's admission catches me off guard.

The only thing is, I made a promise to Coach Lawson. I nod silently, clinking my glass against his, acknowledging the unspoken bond between us, and take a sip, letting the warmth of the moment chase away the chill of ghosts from our pasts.

The low hum of conversation and the music from the jukebox fade into the background as Jamie's gaze meets mine. His eyes hold a sincerity that makes my heart flutter unexpectedly.

"Really, Lara, it's great that you're on our team. You're a step up from Dr. Andrews."

I smile. "Really?"

"Cuter, too."

"Ha," I say. Considering Dr. Andrews was four feet tall and looked like a weasel, it's not much of a compliment.

"No, but I mean it." Jamie's voice is earnest, threaded with an emotion that resonates within me. "You get it, you know? It's like I can drop the weight of expectations when you're around."

I lean back in my seat, the leather creaking softly under me, and study him for a moment. There's something about Jamie that's so different from the others—the way he carries himself, the careful consideration behind his words. He's more than just a talented athlete; he's someone who feels deeply, who values connection over accolades.

"With all the guys, it's posturing, who can be the biggest wolf. With women, they treat me like I'm some celebrity. But I'm neither. It's easy to be myself with you," he continues, and there's a vulnerability in his admission that tugs at me. "It's a relief, actually."

I smile, warmth spreading through my chest. It's not just his gratitude that wraps around me—it's the trust he's offering, the unguarded honesty that's so rare in our world of competitive sports.

"Jamie, I—" The words catch in my throat as our eyes lock. Something shifts between us, a silent recognition of the bond that's been forming, fragile yet undeniable.

"Hey," he says softly, his hand reaching across the table to cover mine, his touch gentle but firm. "How about we do this again? Not in a bar, not after practice. Somewhere... neutral. You know, outside of work."

My pulse quickens at the suggestion, at the prospect of exploring whatever this is without the constraints of our professional roles. I think of the hours spent analyzing injuries, formulating recovery plans—all important, but suddenly there's this, something personal and promising that beckons with every shared glance and word.

"I'd like that," I say, my voice steady despite the excitement that flutters in my stomach. A date, I realize. We're talking about a real date.

"Great." He grins, and the lightness in his expression makes him even more attractive, if that's possible. "How does Saturday sound? Maybe we can walk by the beach."

I open my mouth to agree, already picturing the orange hues reflecting on the water, the soft sand beneath our feet. But more than that, I envision the quiet conversations, the laughter, the chance to see Jamie away from the ice—away from the pressures that define our daily lives.

Then I remember what I told myself, and what I promised Lawson. Professional. I have to be professional. That means no romantic entanglements, even with gorgeous, wonderful men like Jamie. "Wait—I'm sorry. I can't. I probably shouldn't even be here with you. You see...I feel like I kind of made a promise to Coach Lawson that I'd stay focused on my job. And so I want to keep things purely professional. I have to make a good impression this first season, so she'll hire me back next season."

His face falls. "Oh. Okay. No problem," he says coolly. He motions to the door. "We definitely don't want to send Lawson on a warpath. That could be bad. I guess we should probably get going."

I hate that I put a damper on the first real, good conversation I've had with a guy in forever. But I can't help it. My job means everything to me. I follow him out the door quietly.

The cool night air kisses my skin as we walk. Jamie's car is up ahead, a silent witness to the tentative steps we're taking toward something new, something potentially life-changing. I can't help but feel that each step forward is also a step into the unknown.

"Thanks for tonight, Lara," he says, his voice a quiet echo in the evening stillness. "It means a lot."

"Thank you, Jamie. For opening up to me." My heart throbs with a mix of emotions—excitement, nervousness, and an unexpected fear of what comes next. The professional boundaries that once defined our interactions are blurring, and with that shift comes a tide of uncertainties.

As we reach his car, Jamie leans against it, his figure bathed in the soft glow of the streetlights. He hesitates, a shadow of doubt flickering across his face. "I'm sorry if I overstepped my bounds. I don't want to make things difficult for you at work."

"It's okay."

He nods. "Good night, Lara."

I watch him drive away, the red taillights receding into the distance like a metaphor for my life. Stop. Caution. Be careful. Don't let your heart get stuck.

Not yet, anyway. One year. Once I've secured a long-term contract with the Titans, maybe I can let down my guard.

But we're talking about gorgeous Jamie Duncan, who can melt my heart with a simple smile. If I had a checklist of everything I'm looking for in a guy, he'd tick all the boxes—sweet, good-looking, athletic, good sense of humor. I can already tell that resisting the urge to jump in full force is going to be hard.

CHAPTER FOUR

The echo of my sneakers on the tile is the only sound accompanying me into the locker room. It's supposed to be an empty space at this hour, a rare pocket of calm before the storm of practice. Yet there he is, Wes Carter, "Wild" Wes as they dub him—slumped over his open locker like a marionette with cut strings.

Oh no. The back of my neck prickles with anxiety. Ever since he called me sweetheart and looked at me like his prey, I've been steering clear of him. Everything about him rubs me the wrong way, including the fact that he now smells like a brewery. What the hell has he been up to?

"Hey, Wes?" My voice bounces off the lockers, too loud in the stillness. No response. I stride over, urgency replacing curiosity, because even from here, I can see the pallor of his skin and the way his head rests heavily against the cool metal. The signs are all too familiar, a remnant of college days I'd rather forget.

I reach out, fingers brushing over the fabric of his jersey before settling on his shoulder. There's a firmness underneath, the solid build of a forward who spends more time on ice than anywhere else. I give him a gentle shake, the movement causing his head to loll sideways, revealing bloodshot eyes that struggle to focus.

"Wes," I say again, firmer this time. My role as a sports therapist kicks in despite the early hour and the fact that Wes Carter is the last person I expect to find my care landing upon. But seeing anyone in this state tugs at professional heartstrings I can't ignore. He groans, a low sound that tells me he's definitely going to need more than a few electrolytes to skate through today's practice.

And I should probably tell Lawson. He's seriously jeopardizing his career. But ratting out a member of the team isn't a way to get on its good side, especially this early in *my* career.

"Come on, Carter. Practice in thirty. You know better than this," I chide, crossing my arms over my chest. My professional concern is morphing into irritation because Wes Carter, of all people, should understand the stakes.

He groans and lifts his head, squinting against the harsh fluorescent lighting of the locker room. "I'm fine, sweetheart," he mutters, trying to brush me off with a wave of his hand. "Just a rough night."

There it is, that easy, slow drawl that has worked its way into my thoughts more times than I care to admit. As much as I hate to be called sweetheart, there's something in the timbre of his voice that's utterly magnetic.

"Fine?" My voice rises incredulously as I take in his disheveled appearance. "You look like you've been steamrolled by the Zamboni." I lean closer, driven by a mix of frustration and the innate need to help. "You're an athlete, Wes. Your body isn't just yours; it's an investment for the team, for your career."

Wes scoffs, pushing himself up to sit straighter on the bench. His movements are sluggish, but there's a fire kindling in those bleary eyes now. "Dr. Lara Bennett, preaching about the sanctity of the season," he drawls sarcastically. "I've been playing hockey since I could walk. I think I know how to handle a little hangover."

"Knowing how to handle a hangover isn't the point," I retort, hands landing on my hips. My ponytail swings as I shake my head at him, the motion no doubt emphasizing my exasperation. "It's about respecting the game, respecting yourself enough to not let it get to this point. I mean, what would Coach say if she saw you like this? You need to get something in you to sober you up."

He gives a dry laugh, and it's like watching the bad boy facade slip back into place. "Your modern methods and sports science sermons aren't necessary here, sweetheart." Wes stands, towering over me now, his expression defiant. "I don't need you or anyone else telling me how to take care of myself."

As we stand face-to-face, I can feel the tension thickening, electrified, like the charged silence before a thunderstorm. There's a flicker of something in his gaze, a defiance that pulls at me, challenging and intense. Our breath mingles in the small space between us, and I'm acutely aware of the heat radiating from his body despite the chill of the room.

"Is that so?" I barely recognize my own voice, dipped in a cocktail of anger and something more dangerous. Something that makes my heart skip a beat as I meet his stare, unflinching. "Your bloodshot eyes say differently. And you smell gross."

He chuckles, a low, throaty sound. "But admit it. You want me anyway."

My eyes go wide. He didn't just say that, did he? But there's no doubt he's very used to being wanted. I saw that during the first game, when there were dozens of groupies in CARTER jerseys lined up outside the locker room. He could've had his pick.

"Your silence implies consent," he says, clearly amused. "So here's what I'm proposing. We can go back to that table of yours and have a little fun."

My jaw drops.

An easy smile spreads over his beautiful face. "I think the words you are searching for are *go to hell*?"

We're caught in a standoff, inches apart, the air around us crackling with an energy that has nothing to do with our argument. It's a moment suspended in time, where the line between irritation and attraction blurs, leaving me breathless with anticipation.

"Or maybe you're a bad girl in a good girl's body, and you're game." He reaches out, natural as can be, and pushes a lock of my hair that has escaped the ponytail behind my ear. "Not going to deny it, I see."

Is he out of his mind? Too full of liquid courage to even see that he's way out of line?

"Oh, yes I am. You're disgusting," I tell him. "Take a shower. Maybe it'll wake you up for practice."

Before I can turn away, he grabs my wrist.

Time stands perilously still, and I'm all but lost in the depths of Wes's eyes. The intensity that radiates from his gaze is equal parts unnerving and intoxicating, daring me to cross a line I can't even see anymore. What is wrong with me? He's a jerk. I should be able to stop this.

But before I can shake him off, the harsh creak of the locker room door slicing through the silence shatters the moment into fragments. My head snaps toward the sound, and Wes's body tenses beside me as Jamie steps into the room, halting abruptly. His eyes widen—a striking contrast against his light hair—surprise etched starkly across his features.

"Hey..."

His voice trails off, unfinished, as if the rest of his question lingers somewhere in the suddenly stifling air of the locker room. I step back from Wes, my pulse hammering away in my throat, cheeks ablaze with a heat that has nothing to do with the temperature of the room.

“Jamie,” I manage, though my voice sounds like it belongs to someone else, weak and far too high. I watch him closely, seeing how his jaw tightens, the subtle shift in his stance that speaks volumes of the discipline he embodies. How different he is from Wes, how much simpler things should be with him.

He looks at Wes, his expression hardening further, and for a brief moment, no one speaks. The tension between them is palpable, seeming to manifest physically in the space that separates them. It feels like standing on the edge of a precipice, the wind threatening to push us into an abyss we can’t escape.

“Didn’t mean to interrupt,” Jamie finally says, though his voice holds an edge that tells me he sees more than he wants to, more than I wish he could. There’s history there, in the way he squares his shoulders, the memory of a confrontation not so long ago lingering like a shadow between the two men.

I clear my throat, trying to find my footing again, to remember who I am—the sports therapist who knows better, who should act better. But the flustered embarrassment clings to me, refusing to be shaken off so easily. I know how this must look. Wasn’t I just telling Jamie I wanted to keep things professional? And here I was, almost drawn in by those wicked eyes. I look between the two of them, the good guy and the bad boy, the former with his quiet strength, the latter with his wild defiance.

“You weren’t interrupting anything. Practice starts soon,” I say, my voice steadier now but still lacking conviction. “You two should get ready.”

It’s a feeble attempt to restore normalcy to a situation that’s anything but normal. Jamie watches me for a heartbeat longer, searching my face for something I can’t quite decipher. Then, without another word, he turns his attention to his locker, the pointed silence hanging heavy around us. Wes runs a hand through his hair, ruffled and unruly, his smirk gone as he watches Jamie’s back.

The complexity of this triangle tightens around us, constricting and confusing. And as I stand there, caught between the two men who represent such contrasting choices, I can’t help but wonder how I’ll ever navigate through the labyrinth of emotions they’ve both come to evoke in me.

“See you later, sweetheart,” Wes says, making me cringe as he grabs his shave kit and saunters away, toward the showers. I don’t mistake Jamie’s back tensing as he hunches over his locker.

I fidget from one foot to the other, the rubber soles of my trainers squeaking against the tiled floor—an awkward soundtrack to the palpable tension. My gaze flits from Jamie's furrowed brow to Wes's disheveled form, and I feel at a loss for words. This isn't a scene from some tawdry romance novel; this is my life unraveling in real time.

I need to say something.

"Jamie, it's not—" My voice trembles, betraying the turmoil swirling inside me. Not what it looks like? Then what was it? A knot forms in my stomach, tightening with every silent second that ticks by. Guilt gnaws at the edges of my consciousness, confusion dances across my thoughts, and beneath it all, an unwelcome current of attraction still hums.

"Hey. You don't have to explain," he says, not looking at me.

But then why do I feel like I do?

"He was just hung over, and I was trying to help him."

Jamie nods. I see doubt in his eyes.

"Look, I should really…" There's so much I want to say, but nothing feels right. The explanations lodge stubbornly in my throat, and I can't muster the force to dislodge them. "I'll see you out on the ice."

With a faint nod, more to myself than to him, I turn away. My fingers fumble over the zipper of my sports bag as I pack away my tape and water bottle, each item echoing like a gavel judging my actions. My cheeks still burn with the heat of what almost happened, and I'm acutely aware of every breath, every shift in their stance.

"Sorry," I murmur. That was what I had wanted to say, because even though nothing happened, if Jamie hadn't come in, I'm afraid it would have. And it feels like a betrayal, after what we'd talked about at the bar. The word is swallowed by the thick silence. Without another glance, I sling my bag over my shoulder—its weight suddenly feeling like the burden of my own indecision—and push through the heavy door, heading for the rink.

The cool corridor air greets me, but it does little to soothe the firestorm behind my ribcage. Every step away from the locker room is laden with uncertainty, my heart pounding a staccato rhythm against my chest. What am I doing? What do I want?

As I walk, the questions multiply, branching out into endless possibilities, none of which I'm ready to face. I've always prided myself on being level-headed, on knowing my path, but now… Now I'm not just caught between two very different guys I'm really attracted to—I'm lost in a maze of my own making, with no clear way out.

CHAPTER FIVE

I peel off the last strip of athletic tape from the dispenser, securing it around the ankle of the forward who grumbles about the day's rough scrimmage. "That should do it," I say, ushering him out with a pat on his shoulder. As he limps away, the quiet of the therapy room settles over me like a dense fog, and my gaze drifts to the schedule clipped to the clipboard.

Wes Carter. Last on the list.

Perfect.

My heart hammers against my ribcage as I contemplate the impending solitude, Wes and I alone in the clinical coolness of this room. A thrill races down my spine, tangled up with a thread of apprehension that tightens with each second ticking by on the clock. Wes is... complicated. Charismatic in a way that seems to bypass reason and resonate directly with the senses.

"Professionalism," I remind myself, the word a talisman against the simmering attraction I've fought so hard to ignore. The athletes depend on me, trust me to keep their bodies game-ready. It's not just a job—it's my calling, my salvation after my own dreams of sprinting glory were snatched away by one misstep, one crack of bone.

"Alright, Wes, you're up," I call out, mustering every ounce of clinical detachment I can summon. The door swings open, and there he stands, all cocky grin and unruly curls—a man who wears rebellion as comfortably as his well-worn leather jacket.

"Evening, Lara," he says, sauntering in. His voice is a smoky baritone that curls around my name like a caress. "Hope you saved the best for last."

"Let's keep things professional, Wes," I reply, but my pulse betrays me, thrumming faster at his proximity. He chuckles, a low sound that seems to vibrate through the space between us.

"Always professional," he agrees, though his eyes glint with mischief as he takes a seat on the therapy table, his movements fluid and assured.

"Shoulder still giving you trouble?" I ask, approaching with guarded steps. Our work has brought us physically close before—too close—not that I'd ever let him know how it affects me.

"Nah," he replies, rolling his shoulder in demonstration. The movement causes his T-shirt to tighten across his chest, and I force my attention back to my task.

"Alright, take off your shirt. Let's see what we're dealing with." The words are brusque, professional, but they hang heavy in the air, charged with an energy I dare not acknowledge.

"Your wish is my command," he teases, pulling the fabric over his head in one smooth motion, revealing a canvas of tanned skin and defined muscle that speaks of hours spent training. He has two full sleeves of tattoos, and one of a symbol I don't recognize on his left pectoral. I suppress the urge to ask him what it means, because that seems too personal. I catch a whiff of his cologne, something woodsy and warm, and it's like a punch to the senses.

Focus, Lara, I chide myself silently, laying my hands on his shoulders, trying to ignore the heat radiating from his skin. My fingers probe expertly for signs of injury, yet I'm acutely aware of his every breath, the faintest shift in his posture.

"How's that feel?" My voice doesn't waver, but inside, a storm brews.

"Better already," he murmurs, flashing a roguish smile that doesn't quite reach his eyes. There's tension there, a flicker of something deeper, but I can't—won't—pursue it.

"Good," I manage, stepping back to maintain a semblance of distance. "Keep it steady. No sudden movements."

"Wouldn't dream of it," he replies, but the tilt of his lips suggests otherwise. There's a dance we're doing here, one of words and glances, and I'm suddenly unsure of the steps. Wes has always been a wildcard, but tonight, in the dim light of the therapy room, he's magnetic in a way that threatens to pull me under.

The air is thick with tension, and the low hum of the therapy equipment only amplifies the current of electricity between Wes and me. His presence looms large in the small room, his aura of confidence and rebellion feeling like a tangible force pressing against my professional boundaries.

"Steady?" I ask, my voice barely above a whisper, as I adjust the straps on his shoulder, feigning a focus that's constantly threatened by his proximity.

"Always," Wes says, and there's an edge to his voice that sounds like a challenge. He's close enough that I can see the dark lashes framing those mischievous eyes, feel the warmth radiating from his body. His casual arrogance is a siren's call, and I'm desperately trying not to crash upon the rocks.

Just then, the sound of the door creaking open shatters the moment, and I whirl around, pulse racing. My movement is too abrupt, and I collide with a solid chest in a hockey jersey, arms flailing for balance.

"Whoa there, Lara," Jamie says, steadying me with hands that are both gentle and firm. His face is red from exertion and there's a sheen of sweat on his brow. "Didn't mean to startle you."

"Jamie," I breathe out, surprised. This is the second time in a week he's caught me in a compromising position with Wes. But even though I tell myself my hands being on Wes's chest is purely professional, a flush of embarrassment heats my cheeks.

Jamie's eyes flicker with concern, and I can't help but notice how his blond hair falls just right, even after what must have been hours on the ice.

"Working late?" My words feel clumsy, tripping over the silence that Wes has left hanging heavy in the room.

"Practicing those drills," Jamie replies, his grin apologetic yet proud. There's a dedication in his stance, a quiet strength that contrasts sharply with Wes's brash charm.

"Yeah," Wes cuts in, voice smooth as silk, clearly unimpressed. "That's Jamie. Always teacher's pet."

"You're only saying that because of the number of times the teacher makes you stand in the corner, Wes," Jamie replies, polite but with a tightness around his eyes. He turns back to me, and there's a question there, something unspoken that tugs at my insides.

"Sorry, I didn't realize you were still working. I'll get out of your hair," Jamie adds, but he doesn't move, his gaze lingering for a second too long.

"Actually, we're just finishing up," I say, unsure why the words feel like a betrayal. Wes raises an eyebrow, a silent challenge in his expression.

"Right." Jamie nods stiffly, though he doesn't budge. There's a beat of awkward silence where no one seems willing to break eye contact or leave the room first.

"What?" Wes starts with a mock pout at me, leaning back on the therapy bed with an ease that suggests he owns the place. "How about that full-body massage you were telling me about?"

Jamie's eyes narrow. Horrified, I slam my hand into Wes's bad shoulder. "Ha!" I erupt, too loud.

He winces in pain. "I'll take that as a no," he groans. "Ah, I thought you were supposed to make it feel better."

"Sorry!" I cringe, feeling like the worst physical therapist ever. I'm *supposed* to make them feel better, not worse.

"I'll forgive you if you massage it." He gives me a pleading look.

I've had just about enough of his games. I scowl at him.

"I'll let you two go," Jamie mumbles, his voice softening as he looks at me. "Wouldn't want to disrupt the healing process."

"Disruption" feels like a gross understatement for the maelstrom of emotions swirling inside me. Both men stand in the room, their contrasting energies creating a vortex that threatens to consume me whole.

"Goodnight then," Wes says, the word sounding more like a velvet purr than a farewell. Jamie gives a short nod and finally steps out, closing the door behind him with a quiet click that resonates like a gavel.

"Where were we?" Wes asks, the corner of his mouth lifting in an all-knowing smirk as he turns his attention back to me.

"No massage," I reply firmly, pulling myself together as I step away to create some much-needed distance. The room feels smaller now, the air somehow both emptier and denser without Jamie.

A hush falls over the room that's louder than any words. My pulse races, my mind replays Jamie's retreat—the way his eyes lingered with an intensity that belied his composed exit. I lean against the cool wall for a second, allowing myself the briefest pause. Wes's presence behind me is like a live wire; I can almost feel the hum of his energy in the space between us.

"Everything okay?" His voice holds a note of genuine concern beneath the teasing edge, and it grates on my nerves how he manages to sound so unaffected.

"Fine," I reply, straightening. The word feels brittle on my tongue, a stark contrast to the whirlwind of emotions I'm desperately trying to tamp down. "I'm just trying to keep professional."

"And I'm not making it easy." He arches an eyebrow, and there's a glint of something in his gaze that sends a shiver down my spine.

"That's okay. You're not the first good girl to give in to her primal urges where I'm concerned."

"I'm not having any primal urges!" I practically shout at him, folding my arms defensively across my chest. My face heats. It feels like a lie. Otherwise, why would he have me so worked up? "Stop being disgusting and let me do my work."

"Fine, fine. I'm sorry. I was just joking." He holds his hands up in surrender.

"It wasn't funny."

There's a silence then, a heavy moment where we both seem to acknowledge the unspoken feelings tangling the air.

"Jamie's a good guy," Wes says after a beat, his voice unusually soft. I'm taken aback by the sincerity in his tone.

"Yeah, he is." It's all I can manage without giving too much away. I have to remind myself of the lines drawn around us—lines of professionalism, of boundaries not meant to be crossed. But Jamie's dedication, his quiet strength, they resonate with a part of me that yearns for something more than just fleeting moments.

"I can tell you like him," he continues, as I wonder where he's heading.

"I do. I like all the players," I say, trying to be diplomatic.

"Yeah. I get it. But I bet none of them have ever made your heart race quite like I do, though." Wes's cheeky grin is back in place, and it's as if the emotional weight of our conversation evaporates under his playful scrutiny.

"Let's get back to work," I deflect, ignoring the flutter in my stomach. "We've got progress to make."

"Lead the way, Coach." He winks, and I can't help but roll my eyes even as a reluctant smile tugs at my lips.

I guide Wes through his exercises, hyperaware of each brush of skin, every shared breath. There's an intimacy here that goes beyond the physical proximity required by therapy. It's in the trust he places in me, in the careful control I exert over each movement. Wes might play the bad boy, but underneath, when he lets the mask slip, there's a vulnerability that catches me off guard.

"Thanks, Lara," he murmurs as he completes a particularly grueling set. "You know, for pushing me."

"It's what I'm here for," I say, my voice steadier than I feel.

He studies me for a moment, his expression unreadable. "You're good at this. At getting under people's skin."

So are you. I swallow hard, unsure how to take his comment. "Only to help them heal."

"Right." He nods, slow and deliberate. "Healing."

The session ends with a palpable tension that lingers long after he leaves. Alone in the quiet aftermath, I find my thoughts drifting back to Jamie. His steadfast gaze, the warmth in his voice, the unassuming manner that seems to see right through me. And Wes, with his inexplicable allure and unexpected depth, unsettling my balance in ways I hadn't anticipated.

As I lock up the therapy room, the weight of the evening's complexities settles heavily on my shoulders. I've always been good at keeping my personal feelings separate from my professional life, but now, as I flick off the lights and step into the darkened corridor, I'm not so sure anymore.

There's no denying the draw I feel toward both men, each pulling me in a different direction when I need to stay firmly in the middle. Wes, with his challenge to the steadiness I've built around myself, and Jamie, whose sincerity echoes my own hidden desires. But I can't be pulled in by either of them. I push open the entrance doors to the night air, taking a deep breath to clear my head.

I'll need to navigate these waters carefully. Whatever lies ahead, one thing is certain: My world has shifted, and there's no going back to the simplicity of before.

CHAPTER SIX

The cold press of the stethoscope against Ethan's chest brings a familiar sense of purpose to my movements. "Deep breath," I instruct, my hands deftly working over the contours of bruised ribs, gauging the severity through touch and sound. The training room is my domain, a world away from the roar of the ice rink, where twinges and aches are nursed back to battle-readiness under my watchful eye. It's also my refuge from the two men I've been thinking about more than I'd like to admit, since they're both healthy and not on my clipboard today.

"Looks like you'll live, Captain," I quip, offering a half-smile as I secure an ice pack to his side. "But take it easy for a couple of days."

Ethan nods, relief mingling with respect in his eyes. He steps out into the gym, joining the others. My job isn't just about healing; it's about instilling confidence, ensuring these warriors on ice trust their bodies to withstand the next clash.

Amidst the clatter of weights and the hum of treadmills, I catch a glimpse of myself in the mirror. Auburn hair pulled back, eyes focused, I'm the image of dedication—a far cry from the sprinter who never crossed her final finish line. Pride floods in. Here I am, minding my very own semi-pro hockey team. Every success here is a balm to that old wound I'd gotten on the track.

As I scribble down some notes, the door swings open with a force that slices through the steady rhythm of the room. Pat Lawson steps inside, her presence commanding immediate silence. Coach Lawson, a snake in human form, always seems coiled and ready to strike. Today, her glare fixates on me, and I brace for impact.

"Care to explain your latest experiment, Bennett?" Her voice is sharp, each word a pointed barb. There's no mistaking the challenge in her tone.

"Which one?" I ask, feigning innocence. My heart beats a little faster, but I keep my face composed. This isn't my first tango with skepticism.

"Your so-called 'cutting-edge' recovery technique, giving Smith that splint and then putting him back on the ice? You're not in a lab, you're dealing with real players here." Pat's accusation hangs heavy in the air.

I sigh. I chose Northern University because it was at the forefront of sports medicine, using new methods that had been proven to be much more effective, cutting recovery times in half, or even allowing athletes to compete at peak *with* an injury, without adversely affecting their health. I'd wanted to learn those methods because it felt like the wave of the future. But Lawson subscribes to Dr. Andrews's traditional way of thinking. She's not just resistant to change, she's clearly against it, no matter what results I show.

"With all due respect," I say, keeping a smile pasted on my face, "you hired me for my expertise and professional judgment, and that's what I'm trying to—"

"Correction: The *board* hired you," she seems to take great pleasure in telling me. "There are ten of us on that board, and it wasn't unanimous. Both Dr. Andrews and I weren't convinced you were the right person for the job."

The words hit me like a ton of bricks. She voted against me? And Dr. Andrews did too? I fight to keep my composure.

"That's fine. I look forward to proving to you that I can handle this assignment. And I don't make rash decisions. I research thoroughly before applying any new method," I reply, standing firmly amidst the jungle of medical equipment. "Everything I do is to minimize recovery time and maximize performance."

"Or maximize risk?" she counters quickly, her eyes scanning the room, daring others to join her inquisition. "Smith might hurt himself worse, being put on the ice so soon."

"Coach, Smith is going to be just fine. Did he complain once? Every treatment I've introduced has been vetted. There's science and success behind them," I insist, but my assurance flickers like a candle in a storm. She's questioning my competence in front of the whole team—my team.

"Science," she scoffs. "I've seen more injuries this season than the last two combined. Coincidence?"

I want to argue, to defend my methods that have helped countless athletes before. Especially since I know part of the reason there have been so many injuries is because Wes and T-Rex and players like them take more risks than most hockey players do. But Pat's reputation precedes her—a titan of tradition in a sport that reveres its old ways. And here I am, trying to rewrite the playbook.

The room feels smaller, the walls festooned with championship banners now witnesses to my trial by fire. Team members avert their gazes, discomfort etched into their faces. They rely on both of us—Pat for direction, me for healing—and I can't tell if they're hoping for my vindication or my downfall.

"Your 'innovations' could be compromising our players, Bennett. Maybe even the season." Pat's words are a gut punch, and a ripple of tension passes through the onlookers. "But I suppose the proof will be in the pudding. We'll just have to see."

"Undermining" would be a gentler term, but she chooses "compromising" with all its implications. I feel the weight of her doubt, the insinuation that I might be dangerous. It's a master class in undermining without uttering the word directly.

"You *will* see. Every player I treat gets back on the ice stronger," I say, though my conviction wanes. The assurance with which I began this conversation is slipping through my fingers like sand.

"Stronger, or just patched up enough to break down again?" Pat presses on, relentless.

I search the room for an ally, someone who believes in my work, who understands that progress sometimes means pushing boundaries. Silence answers me, and in it, I hear my own faltering heartbeat. Maybe it's pride or the ghost of my sprinter's spirit that keeps me grounded, refusing to let me flee. But as Pat Lawson's shadow looms larger, my desire to escape grows, even as I stand my ground.

I square my shoulders, forcing myself to meet Pat's accusatory gaze. "I feel like I'm helping them."

"Feel?" Pat scoffs, her eyes narrowing. "You're experimenting on our team, Lara. These aren't lab rats; these are athletes with careers on the line."

The room seems to contract, the walls inching closer as if to press the breath from my lungs. A few of the players shift uncomfortably, their glances flickering between Pat and me. I can almost feel their skepticism, a tangible presence that threatens to smother my resolve.

"Everything I do is for their benefit," I insist, but the vibrancy of my defense is dimming, corroded by doubt. The unspoken question hangs heavy in the air: What if she's right? What if in my zeal to innovate, I've jeopardized more than just my reputation?

"Benefit?" Pat retorts, her voice rising. "It's a fine line, one you might have already crossed. But like I said, we'll just have to wait and see the results."

My mouth opens, yet no sound emerges. Rage creeps up my neck, a flush that feels like a brand. I want to argue, to stand tall against the onslaught, but it's clear words won't convince this woman. I need to show results. That's the only thing that will satisfy her.

All around us, eyes watch, ears listen, and judgments form.

"Hey, wait," a firm voice cuts through the tension, and I nearly sag with relief as I turn to see Jamie, his height commanding attention as he moves to place himself between Pat and me. His expression is resolute, his eyes like chips of ice against the heat of the argument.

"Coach, that's pretty harsh," Jamie says evenly. "Lara's methods—they work. Hell, they more than work. I'm proof of that. She had Ethan take a break after his wrist was showing signs of strain. And he was back on the ice in days. Andrews probably would've let him play until it broke, which would've kept him out half the season."

I put up a hand. "Jamie, thanks, but I can handle thi—"

"No, Lara. It's true." He motions vaguely toward the people in the gym. "Look at them. Look at me. Last season, I was benched more often than not, nursing one injury after another. This year? I've been on the ice every game, playing better than ever. It's all thanks to Lara. She doesn't just patch us up; she makes us stronger."

His words hang in the air, a counterweight to Pat's accusations. I watch as her face softens, her doubt melting into something that looks like respect—or at least reconsideration.

"Her techniques aren't conventional, sure," Jamie continues, "but since when has progress followed convention? She's committed to our health and our success. Isn't that what we all want?"

For a moment, there's silence—a hush of contemplation. Then, like the first thaw of spring, she nods. The tension that had been suffocating me loosens its grip, and I draw in a deep, steadying breath.

Jamie turns back to me, his gaze meeting mine with unwavering support. "Lara, your work speaks for itself. And I, for one, am grateful."

I want to fight my own battles. I wasn't put on this hockey team to let men defend my honor. Even so, gratitude wells up within me, mingling with a sense of camaraderie that I hadn't realized I'd missed so acutely. In Jamie's defense, I find a renewed sense of purpose, a reminder of why I push the boundaries—for athletes like him, who carry the same fire that once burned in me.

The training room slowly empties, the buzz of earlier conversations replaced by a quiet that feels like a balm to my frayed nerves. Jamie lingers, gathering his gear, but his movements are unhurried—a deliberate pause in a day that's spun out of control. The lingering team members toss him curious glances because they obviously heard him defending me, but he seems oblivious to them, his focus narrowed to the space between us.

"Thank you," I start, my voice not quite steady. I cross the space, closing the distance that minutes ago felt insurmountable. "You didn't need to, but I appreciate it."

He looks up, the blue of his eyes clear and intense, a stark contrast to the muddled chaos Pat left in her wake. "You don't need to thank me, Lara." His tone is gentle, yet there's an undercurrent of conviction that resonates deep within me. "I meant every word."

"Still," I insist, feeling the heat rise to my cheeks—not from embarrassment this time, but from a warmth that blooms within me, spreading through my chest and making my heart beat faster. "It was brave. Going against Lawson? You didn't have to put yourself out there for me."

"Ah, she looks like a dragon, but she's a teddy bear at heart," he says with a shrug that doesn't quite disguise the tension in his shoulders. "Besides, I know what it's like to be on the receiving end of doubt—to have people question your methods, your commitment." He pauses, and I see something flicker in his gaze. Understanding, maybe. Or recognition.

"Your support—it means everything," I admit, and the sincerity in my own voice surprises me.

Jamie's smile is slow but genuine, reaching his eyes and softening the edges that moments before seemed so sharp. "We're on the same team, Lara. We want the same things." He hesitates, then adds, "And I trust you. With my career, with my health. That's not something I take lightly."

His trust anchors me, a solid presence in the shifting sands of my professional life. And in that moment, I realize how much I've come to rely on his quiet strength, his unwavering belief in me—even when I struggle to find it in myself.

The corridors of the facility are dim, most of the staff long gone, their shifts over before the drama unfolded. The echo of our footsteps is a steady rhythm, a backdrop to the thoughts tumbling through my mind.

"Jamie," I say, halting near the exit. He stops too, turning to face me, his expression open and expectant. "About the other night—with Wes—I just wanted to say…"

He waits, patient as always, giving me the space to find the words that tangle on my tongue.

"I got the feeling you thought you were interrupting a moment between us, or something. But nothing's been happening between us," I blurt out, more abruptly than I intended. My hands twist together, knuckles white with the force of my grip. "Whatever it looks like, it's been professional. I wouldn't… like I said, I couldn't."

"I know," he replies simply, and the weight of those two syllables is staggering. There's no trace of doubt, no need for further explanation.

"You do?" I ask, searching his face for signs of uncertainty but finding none.

"Of course." His voice is steady, reassuring. "I believe you. If you tell me something, I believe it. And you're a professional. I know."

"Oh, good," I whisper, the relief washing over me in waves. It's one thing to assert my innocence, another entirely to be believed without question. "I just felt like these past few days, you've been looking at me differently."

"Nah," Jamie says softly, stepping closer. His hand lifts, fingers brushing against mine in a fleeting touch that sends a current through me. "I'm here for you. As a friend. And if you ever want to, you know…"

He trails off, but his gaze holds mine—a promise unspoken.

The silence stretches between us, heavy and laden with a thousand unspoken words. But it feels comfortable. I've dated guys before, briefly, but never felt so relaxed around a man before. Jamie's presence is a balm to the raw edges of my anxiety, soothing the turmoil that Pat's confrontation ignited within me. The honesty in his eyes anchors me, holding me fast when I might otherwise drift into a sea of self-doubt.

"I appreciate that, Jamie. Maybe we can go out for a couple of beers and catch a game at McGinty's?" I say, speaking solely as a friend.

"Yeah. That sounds good. Hit me up whenever you want to. Take care, okay, Lara?" he says sincerely as he turns to leave.

The warmth in my chest flares at his words, my heart skipping a beat. There is so much tenderness in everything he says to me, so much honesty. He believes in me, stands by me, and that means so much right now, when I'm fighting to prove myself to this team. It's a testament to

Jamie's character, to the core values that make him who he is—disciplined, dedicated, genuine.

"Yes, thanks," I call after him. "You, too."

I think about him all during my ride home. There's wisdom in his simplicity, in the way he sees the world. It's easy to imagine leaning on Jamie, trusting in the steadiness he exudes. As much as I want to stay professional, my friendship with Jamie feels like the first page of something new, something potentially wonderful.

But next year. I have to wait. I have a commitment to the Titans, to see this season through, no matter what challenges Coach Lawson throws at me.

CHAPTER SEVEN

The raucous cheers of the crowd at Happy Dan's pub echo off the walls, amplifying the electric charge that hums through the air. We're here in Knoxville for an away game tomorrow afternoon, and the place is a pulsating heart of excitement, each beat a clink of glass or a burst of laughter. I'm right in the middle of it all, perched on a high stool with Jamie beside me, his presence a calm anchor in the tempest of revelry.

"Can you believe this crowd?" I shout over the noise, my voice barely cresting the wave of enthusiasm that floods the place. My gaze sweeps across the sea of faces—all eyes glued to the screens showcasing the latest hockey plays from our rivals.

Jamie nods, but there's a tightness around his eyes that hints at something beyond the casual observation. He fidgets with his drink, the condensation from the glass wetting his fingertips as he spins it absentmindedly. His usual easygoing demeanor is frayed at the edges tonight, his eyes flickering around the room like a skittish colt.

I bite on my lip. He's scaring me. I thought that when I invited him out, he'd understand. I want him as my friend. I *need* friends. But I still need to hold to my promise to Coach Lawson. For the past few weeks, we've been doing a dance, being professional with one another, but even so, we've been getting closer. Try as I might, I can't help the force that's pushing us together, demanding that we be more than just buddies.

"Everything okay?" My question slices through the cacophony, and for a moment, I catch the flicker of vulnerability in his gaze before it's shuttered away.

"Actually, Lara…" His voice trails off, the words getting tangled up somewhere between his brain and his lips.

I lean in closer, my heart hitching a beat as I pick up on his nervous energy. It's unlike Jamie to be so unsettled; he exudes a sense of purpose, a man who knows where he's going and how to get there.

"Jamie?" I prompt, coaxing him to continue. The intensity of his gaze pins me to my spot, and time seems to slow down, the noise of the pub fading into a distant hum.

"I've been meaning to tell you something," he finally admits, the words tumbling out in a rush. "I can't shake this feeling, and I think it's important you know..."

This sounds dangerous. My pulse races, my skin prickling with a mix of anticipation and dread. There's a gravity to his tone that tells me whatever he's about to say will alter the axis on which my world spins.

"Go on," I encourage, my voice a whisper lost in the thunderous applause for a goal scored on screen.

He takes a deep breath, steadying himself. "I know you want to keep things professional, but I like you, Lara. More than a friend. And when I'm out here with you like this, it gets hard."

The confession hits me with the impact of a rogue wave, leaving me momentarily breathless. My eyes lock onto his, searching for any hint of jest, but all I find is raw honesty. Jamie's feelings, once hidden behind the facade of friendship, are now laid bare, shining through the depths of his ocean-blue stare.

"Jamie, I..." Words fail me, my tongue heavy with the weight of emotions I haven't dared to sort through. The practical, assured part of me wants to retreat, to maintain the status quo that's kept my life neatly compartmentalized. But beneath the surface, there's a current of longing that's been stirred, reaching out to entwine with his own quiet yearning.

"I know that's not where you want to go," he says, his voice steady despite the nerves I see dancing in his eyes. "I just needed you to know."

The crowd erupts into another cheer, punctuating the moment with its frenzy. Yet here in our little bubble, the world stands still, waiting for my heart to decide which way the scales will tip.

The din of the pub fades to a dull roar, replaced by the thunderous beating of my own heart. Jamie's gaze holds mine with an intensity that's both terrifying and exhilarating. I lean in, the space between us charged with unspoken words and possibilities.

This is where I'm supposed to reply, but I can't. Words fail me. I inhale sharply, his confession sending ripples through the still waters of my world. My fingertips graze his hand on the table, tentative yet seeking. There's a magnetic pull, an invisible thread drawing us together, and I find myself drowning in those eyes that promise more than just friendship.

"Jamie, I've always…" The words hang in the air, unfinished, as I grapple with the rush of emotions that his proximity invokes—fear, excitement, longing.

"Always what?" he urges gently, his thumb brushing against the back of my hand, grounding me.

"Appreciated you," I finish, though the word feels inadequate to describe the tangle of feelings Jamie has unearthed. I cringe.

"Is that all?" he challenges, a playful edge to his voice that belies the nervous energy emanating from him.

"Maybe not," I admit, a smile tugging at the corners of my mouth, feeling the walls I've built around my heart tremble under his earnest gaze. "I mean, I really like you, too. And I could see us together. But not right now. This job…"

Before either of us can explore this newfound territory further, a sudden crash jolts us apart. My head snaps toward the source of the commotion, the intimacy of our moment shattered by the chaos erupting across the room. A heavy thud of bodies colliding, followed by the unmistakable sound of glass shattering on the hardwood floor, slices through the festive atmosphere.

"Damn it, Wes!" I mutter under my breath, recognizing the familiar figure at the center of the tumult, surrounded by a gaggle of kids in backward baseball caps and polo shirts. Wes, with his untamed dark hair and reckless disposition, is a storm personified, his fists swinging wildly as he stumbles into another patron.

The pub descends into disarray. People shout and scramble away from the brawl, some climbing onto their chairs for a better view, others rushing forward in a futile attempt to intervene. A woman squeals as her drink topples over, spilling its contents like blood across the floor.

"Stay here," I tell Jamie, my voice firm despite the shaking of my hands. The protective instinct, honed from years of caring for athletes on the field, propels me forward. I weave through the crowd, dodging elbows and spilled drinks, my focus singular—to reach Wes before he does something he'll regret.

"Get off me!" Wes roars, his eyes wild with anger and alcohol. He shoves another man, sending him crashing into a nearby table. The impact sends glasses flying, their descent ending in a chorus of crashes that echo through the now-silent pub.

"Wild" Wes is at it again. He may be a force on the ice, but here, amidst the horrified onlookers, he's just another drunken brawler, one misstep away from disaster. And despite the mess of emotions tangling inside me, I can't help but feel a surge of worry for him, for us, for the fragile peace that's been broken in a single, violent moment.

"What's going on?" I demand.

Wes can barely stand up. He points at one of the men, whose lip is bleeding. "This ass-wad thinks Knoxville's going to murder us tomorrow."

His victim wipes at his lip and sneers, "Damn right, pussy." His burly fraternity brother friends nod in agreement. What the hell? Wes was trying to take on five of them, alone?

"Then settle it on the ice!" I shout back.

"Leave me alone," Wes demands, shoving me aside. "I need to take care of this garbage."

Jamie's tall frame cuts through the chaos, his broad shoulders a beacon of calm amidst the tempest. Before I can reach Wes, Jamie has him by the collar, pulling him back with a strength that belies his unassuming nature.

"Enough, Wes!" Jamie's command slices through the din, and for a moment, even the raucous crowd seems to hold its breath.

Wes, however, is having none of it. His face contorts in anger as he shakes off Jamie's grip with a violence that sends shivers down my spine. "Back off, Duncan!" he slurs, swinging a wild, drunken punch at Jamie.

Jamie dodges with an athlete's grace, his eyes never leaving Wes. It's clear he's been in situations like this before, managing to both subdue and protect with an expertise that's unsettlingly attractive.

"Come on, man," Jamie says again, this time with a softer edge, as if trying to reach whatever part of Wes isn't soaked in alcohol and fury. "You need to sober up."

"You have a game tomorrow. Did you forget?" I say.

But Wes ignores me. His pride is wounded, and he snarls, lunging at the frat boy once more. The movement is sloppy, though, and Jamie easily sidesteps, steadying Wes with a firm hand on his shoulder.

"Let's take this outside," Jamie suggests, casting a quick glance over to where I stand, rooted to the spot by concern and something else—admiration for how Jamie handles himself under pressure.

Together, we maneuver Wes out of the pub and into the cool night air. The change of scenery does nothing to sober Wes's rage or his intoxication. But the absence of an audience sees it diminish slowly, like a storm receding into the horizon.

By the time we get to the hotel, Wes is more a stumbling mess than a raging bull, leaning heavily on both Jamie and me. His head lolls forward as we guide him into the elevator, up to his room, and finally onto his bed, where he collapses like a marionette whose strings have been cut.

"Stay with him," Jamie says, brushing a wayward lock from his forehead, his eyes reflecting concern. "I'll grab some coffee. Maybe it'll help sober him up."

"Okay." My throat feels dry watching Jamie stride out of the room. His presence is a comfort, and without him, the space suddenly feels too close, the silence too loud.

"Hey, Lara," Wes mumbles, his voice thick with inebriation. He blinks up at me, his eyes clouded but searching.

"Yeah, Wes?" I approach cautiously, unsure which version of him I'm dealing with now—the angry brawler or the remorseful drunk.

"I know I've been a jerk to you." There's a clumsiness to his words, but also a vulnerability that makes my heart skip a beat. "Thanks for being here for me."

Before I can respond, before I can form any coherent thought, Wes's hand snakes out, grabbing my wrist with a surprising gentleness. He tugs, and I'm falling, landing beside him on the bed. His lips find mine in a whiskey-laced kiss that's both reckless and tender, brimming with an intensity that steals my breath away.

It's wrong, I know it's wrong, but for a fraction of a second, I don't stop him. Because even drunk, his kiss is something I want to get lost in. His taste, the feel of his stubble, all of it awakens a sense inside me that I haven't felt in so long. Then reality rushes back in, and I gently push him away, my heart pounding against my ribs like it wants to escape. Wes's eyes flutter closed, and his grip loosens.

"Sleep it off, Wes," I whisper, my voice betraying the confusion that whirls inside me.

As I sit there, trying to steady my racing pulse, trying to remind myself of everything that just happened and what didn't, the elevator door dings out in the hallway. Footsteps approach. I wipe at my mouth with the back of my hand, my body trembling. The room spins a fraction, the world tilting on its axis as Wes's consciousness fades into the soft oblivion of sleep. His chest rises and falls in an even rhythm beneath my hand, which I notice is still resting there from when I pushed him away. There's a silence now, one that hums with the echo of that kiss—too loud in its quietness.

I'm stunned by my own reaction, by the warmth that spread through me at his touch, the way my body leaned into his before I caught myself. It wasn't supposed to be like this. If I was going to fall for anyone, it would've been Jamie. Wes is insufferable, a real player. He's not the one who makes my heart race with a mere glance or a thoughtful word. That's Jamie's role. And yet, here I am, skin tingling from the brush of lips that definitely did not belong to Jamie.

Confusion knots in my stomach, thick and heavy. My mind races, trying to categorize, to analyze, to understand why I didn't pull away sooner, why part of me didn't want to pull away at all. It's as if a hidden part of me has been unearthed by Wes's unexpected vulnerability, a part I'm not ready to face.

I should feel guilty, should be repulsed by my own hesitation—and I do, but there's something else there too. Something undeniably electric. The realization that I'm beyond attracted to Wes, despite everything, slaps me with the force of a tidal wave, leaving me dizzy and more than a little scared.

"Shouldn't have let it happen," I murmur to the silent room, to the man sleeping off his intoxication, as if the words can somehow undo the confusion he's stirred within me.

The door creaks open, and there's Jamie, every inch the good guy he's always been, carrying a mug of coffee that steams into the cool air of the hotel room. His concerned eyes find mine, and they're filled with questions I'm not sure how to answer.

"Hey," he says softly, approaching with cautious steps. "How's he doing?"

"Passed out," I manage to reply, my voice sounding foreign and distant.

"Good." Jamie nods, setting the coffee down on the nightstand, a safe distance from Wes's slumbering form. "He'll need it when he wakes up."

"Thanks," I whisper, because what else can I say? Thank you for being the kind of person who goes downstairs to get coffee for a man who just tried to punch you? Or thank you for not noticing that I'm sitting here, heart tangled, after kissing another man?

Jamie sits beside me on the bed, his presence comforting and familiar. He looks at Wes, then at me, a frown creasing his brow. "You okay, Lara?" he asks, and it's the concern in his voice that nearly breaks me.

"Yeah, just… tired, I guess." It's a lie, a feeble attempt to mask the storm raging inside me, but it's all I have. "Wondering if I should tell Coach that this is the second time I've seen him drunk. I don't want to be a snitch, but…"

He sucks in a breath. "I don't know. Probably. But I've known him three years and it's never been a problem before."

"Maybe I'll just wait, then."

"Yeah, I'll have a talk with him tomorrow about it when he's sober. Let's get you back to your room," Jamie suggests gently, standing and offering me his hand. It's warm and steady—everything I thought I wanted until a moment of madness made me question it all.

CHAPTER EIGHT

The roar of the crowd reverberates through the arena as I watch from the sidelines, the anticipation thick enough to cut with a knife. The Knoxville Smashers are formidable opponents, their presence on the ice like storm clouds ready to burst. My gaze follows the players, their movements sharp and deliberate, each stride pushing the limits of human agility and strength. I can't help but feel the ghost of adrenaline that used to course through my own veins before a sprint—every muscle coiled, every sense heightened.

I focus on "Wild" Wes Carter. Despite his rough night, he's a force of nature out there, his body moving with an almost reckless abandon that's as mesmerizing as it is concerning. I thought he'd be sloppy, but he's the opposite. There's a tightness in his movements that doesn't speak of his usual fluid grace. Wes is all raw talent and no discipline, a stark contrast to the finely tuned athletes I once aspired to join.

The game is a blur of color and motion until one moment shatters the frenzy into silence. Wes pivots, aiming for a daring maneuver, but instead of the triumphant cheer, there's a collective gasp. My heart lurches as a player crashes full-force into him, and he crumbles onto the ice, his leg buckling beneath him in a way that spells disaster. The arena falls eerily quiet, the absence of sound more alarming than the loudest scream.

Instinct propels me forward, years of training taking over as I rush toward the ice. My therapist's mind catalogs the fall, the unnatural angle, the immediate clutching at his knee—the signs of a serious injury. But my heart worries for Wes, the man behind the bravado, now vulnerable and in pain.

As I slide onto the frigid surface, reaching Wes's side, my hands are steady, but my thoughts are a whirlwind. Could this have been prevented? Did the hangover slow his reflexes, dull his instinctive avoidance of injury? It's not my place to chastise him for his lifestyle choices, yet here we are, the consequence lying between us on the ice.

"Stay still, Wes," I instruct, trying to mask my concern with professional calm. But inside, I'm churning. Every athlete knows the risks, but seeing the aftermath stirs a familiar fear in me, echoing the memory of my own career-ending collision.

Wes grunts, his face twisted in pain, and I work to assess the damage while keeping him still. Ice rushes up to meet my palms, cold and unforgiving, just like the sport we've both dedicated our lives to. As I stabilize his leg, waiting for the medics, guilt gnaws at me. If only he'd taken better care of himself—if only I could have convinced him to. I push the thoughts away, focusing on the man who needs help now, not the mistakes that might have led us here.

The game ends with the Titans losing, 3-0. The locker room is a cacophony of clanks and murmurs, but the undercurrent of tension is palpable as I step inside. My presence, once a source of reassurance to the players, now feels like an intrusion. The air is thick with the smell of sweat and disappointment—Wes's injury has cast a gloom over what should have been a routine game against the Knoxville Smashers.

"This injury is a direct result of your practices, Bennett!" Pat's voice slices through the tumult, sharp and accusing. Her words hit me like a puck to the chest, unexpected and forceful. I turn to face her, meeting the gaze of the head coach, whose steely eyes are hardened with displeasure.

"Pat, you know that's not fair," I reply, my voice firm despite the tremor of surprise. "Wes's injury was unfortunate, but it wasn't due to my methods."

"Unfortunate?" she scoffs, stepping closer, her figure imposing even off the ice. "You're wrong, Lara. They're athletes, not guinea pigs for your new-fangled therapy techniques!"

I feel my cheeks flush with a mixture of anger and defense. Here, in this sanctum of sweat and strategy, my professional integrity is being challenged. I recall the countless hours spent studying each player's physical condition, tailoring programs to their needs, striving to prevent the very injuries we now discuss.

"Every exercise I've introduced is backed by research and designed to minimize risks," I counter, standing my ground. "Wes's lifestyle choices, his… hangover—that's not something I can control."

"Excuses," Pat spits out. "You were hired to keep them healthy, not laid up on a stretcher. Remember that."

This time, there is no one to defend me. I go to the therapy room and shrink into a chair in the corner, burying my head in my hands, fighting the tears. Keep it together, I will myself. Stay professional.

When the tears dry up and I emerge, Coach is gone, but the tension in the locker room is a palpable force, crackling in the air like static before a storm.

Jamie looks up at me with sympathy. "Hey. You're okay. No one blames this on you. That was Wes's own stupid fault."

I give him a look.

"Yeah. Coach might've said a few things, but she was frustrated. This game should've been an easy win. She's pissed because we choked. Wes wasn't at his best because of last night. That's all."

Before I can even begin to feel comforted by those words, Wes, leaning heavily on his crutches, pushes his way through the crowd of hulking figures. His knee, braced and bandaged, sticks out awkwardly, but it's the reckless fire in his eyes that draws my immediate concern.

"Jamie, you think you know everything, huh?" Wes's voice is deceptively calm, the kind of quiet that precedes an avalanche. "We all looked like shit out there. Don't pin this on me. Every single one of us is to blame. Even Lara."

"Cut the crap, Wes," Jamie shoots back, stepping forward until they're nearly chest to chest. His voice is a sharp contrast, a controlled burn against Wes's icy derision. "Lara has nothing to do with your inability to stay upright, on the ice or anywhere else."

"Right, because playing nurse suits her better, doesn't it? Especially when it involves mouth-to-mouth." The smile that curls on Wes's lips is venomous, and time stops.

Everything stops, frozen in time, except I feel a sick lurch in my stomach. I'd hoped that in his drunken state, Wes would have forgotten about it, even though I haven't been able to.

The look on Jamie's face is enough to break my heart. His eyes volley between us. "What the hell are you talking about?"

"Just that she and I had a really nice time last night," he says.

Jamie snorts in disbelief. "Is that before or after you passed out cold?"

But from the look on Jamie's face, the smug smirk on Wes's face, and the icy silence in the room, I can tell the seed that's been planted has taken hold. Now, everyone in the room is wondering if it's true. If I spent last night with Wes.

"Enough!" I interject, stepping between them. The confined space of the locker room makes me feel trapped, caught in the crossfire of their escalating confrontation. It's too late; the damage is done.

"Is that true, Lara?" Jamie's voice is a low rumble, the hurt behind it almost imperceptible. But it's there, and it twists something inside me.

"No. Jamie—" My protest dies on my lips as I see the muscle in his jaw flex, the betraying flicker in his eyes. He looks at me for an answer, and I'm suddenly aware of every pair of eyes in the room fixed on us.

"Really? So you're going to lie, Lara?" Wes challenges. "I thought better of you. Come on, admit it."

All eyes are on me. I can say nothing, do nothing. What kind of mess have I gotten myself into?

"See, it's all over her face," Wes says, the words slung like a weapon. His gaze locks onto mine, challenging, defiant. "Cat got your tongue, Lara? Or were you saving it for another round with—"

"Shut up, Wes!" The words burst from me, sharper and louder than I intended. I look at Jamie, pleading. "Yes, he kissed me. *He* kissed me. When he was drunk. I didn't even know it was happening until…" Oh, god, if this is my excuse, it sounds so stupid. "It meant nothing. Can we please just forget about it?"

"Nothing, huh?" Wes chuffs a humorless laugh, shaking his head. "I bet you haven't been able to stop thinking about it since."

He's onto me. I can feel the weight of silence that follows, heavy with judgment and disbelief. Jamie's shoulders are tense, the lines of his body rigid with restrained emotion. He doesn't say anything, but the disappointment etched into his features speaks volumes. In this instant, I feel a chasm opening between us, one filled with unspoken words and cascading doubts.

"Jamie, please," I plead, reaching out to touch his arm. He flinches, pulling away as if my touch scorches him.

"Don't," he says quietly, and there's a finality to it that sends a shiver down my spine. His gaze shifts from me to Wes, and then to the floor, where his expression hardens. "We'll settle this later."

Wes grins triumphantly, as if he's scored a point in some twisted game. But there are no winners here, only shards of something fragile left scattered across the cold tile floor.

CHAPTER NINE

The smell of antiseptic fills my nostrils as I wrap the last bandage around Wes's knee, which is looking much better than when he first hobbled in last week. He's sprawled on the therapy table like it's a throne, the very picture of athletic arrogance.

"Nice hands, Lara," he says in a tone that could mean anything. "Really. I think you missed your calling. You ever consider a career in massage?" His eyes roam with a certain possessiveness.

But I'm not talking to him. I'm not even *looking* at him. I'm doing my best to finish with him, then shove him out the door.

"Come on, Lara. The least you can do is talk to me after what you did."

My jaw drops. I've been walking on eggshells all week. Does he really have the impudence to suggest I'm responsible for that? "What *I* did? How dare you—"

I stop when I see him smirking at me. This was all his ploy to get me talking to him. Bastard.

I keep my tone level. "Look. I'm just doing my job, Wes. That is all I want to do where you're concerned." My fingers are deft and practiced, moving with an efficiency born from years of training—first for the track, now for this. The transition was never easy, but I found solace in helping others achieve what I no longer could.

"Sure. But you gotta admit, there's something electric between us," he continues, undeterred by my professional demeanor.

"Static electricity, maybe. Annoying and easy to discharge." I finish with his ankle and start packing away the tape and gauze. My movements are precise, my focus resolute. I'm determined not to let him see how his words get under my skin.

"Ouch," he chuckles. "You wound me."

"Only metaphorically, which is an improvement for both of us," I quip back, refusing to look at him. I need to stay detached, uninvolved. Wes Carter, with his wild ways, is a storm I can't afford to get caught up in.

I pack up my things, ready to go. But he lingers. "You'll see yourself out, I hope," I murmur, not looking back as I leave.

Yes, I'm beyond angry at him, as I have been for the past week. It's been difficult tending to him, not just because he keeps throwing one-liners and come-ons my way, suggesting he wants to repeat that kiss, but because ever since then, players have been looking at me like Wes's latest flavor of the month. I don't care so much about that, but the worst thing is, Jamie hasn't said a word to me. And I miss him.

I'm ready to fly out of the parking lot when the pain hits—a white-hot lance through my finger. "Dammit!" I cry out as the car door slams shut on my hand. I'd overreached for the seat belt at the same time I shut the door with my other hand. Panic flares, followed by the sickening throb of crushed flesh.

"Hey! Are you okay?" Jamie's voice cuts through the fog of agony. He's suddenly there, right beside me, his eyes clouded with concern.

My heart does a stutter-step that's more about him than the pain. He's here. Actually talking to me. "I—I think I jammed my finger."

"Let me see," he says softly, reaching for my hand with a gentleness that's the exact opposite of Wes's brashness. Jamie's touch is careful as he examines the swelling digit, his brow furrowed in concentration.

"Thanks, Jamie. I—I'm such a klutz." I attempt a smile, but it's weak, washed out by the pain.

"Don't worry about it. Let's get some ice on that immediately," he replies, helping me out of the car and guiding me back inside with an attentiveness that wraps around me like a warm blanket.

As we walk side by side, I can't help but compare the steadiness of Jamie's presence with the unpredictable whirlwind of Wes. Jamie's reliability should be boring compared to Wes's allure, but in this moment, it's everything I crave.

Inside the locker room, Wes is gone, thank God. Jamie takes me to the table and wraps my injured finger with a practiced care that brings an unexpected comfort. The cold of the ice numbs the throbbing pain, and I let out a sigh.

"Looks like you're not just adept on the ice," I quip, trying to ease the tension knotting my stomach.

"Many talents," he says with a wry smile that doesn't quite reach his eyes. "Ice is only the beginning."

"Should I be scared or impressed?" I tease back, grateful for the distraction. Grateful to be talking to him once again. I want to cry, I missed it so much.

"Definitely impressed." His chuckle warms the sterile air between us, and for a moment, we're just two people sharing a laugh, not two corners of a complicated love triangle.

"Thanks for swooping in. You're like my personal superhero…minus the cape and spandex." I nudge him playfully with my good hand.

"Who says I don't have a cape hidden away? And you need to see me in my Speedo," Jamie counters, a spark of mischief lighting up his eyes.

I giggle. Why do I always have such a good time with him? It's so easy to fall into this rhythm with him, the banter natural and unforced. It reminds me why we connected so well before Wes stormed into the picture.

But as the laughter fades, the weight of my recent actions presses down, and I know I have to address the elephant in the room.

"Jamie…" I start, hesitating. My heart races, but I force myself to meet his gaze. "About that kiss with Wes. It—it was a mistake. I didn't see it coming, and I didn't want it. It just…happened."

He listens, his expression unreadable for a long moment, and I worry I've crossed some invisible line from which there's no return. But then he nods, his face softening.

"Hey, it's okay," he reassures me, his voice gentle. "I know. You said you wanted professional, and I know how persistent Wes can be."

"Yes. But I should've stopped him before—"

"We're human, Lara. Things happen that we don't plan for. I'm not going to hold that against you."

I exhale, relief washing over me like a cleansing rain. Jamie's understanding feels like a balm to the chaos of my thoughts.

"Can we…start over?" I ask tentatively, hope threading through my words.

"Absolutely," he says with a sincere warmth that makes me believe in second chances. "Let's leave the past where it belongs."

In that instant, with Jamie's forgiveness paving the way, I feel lighter, as if a door has opened to a future I wasn't sure was still ours to share.

"Thank you," I say, my voice softer than I intended. My gaze lifts from my bandaged finger to meet his eyes, finding an ocean of understanding there. "Not just for this," I gesture with my wrapped hand, "but for being… you."

Jamie gives me one of his half-smiles, the kind that always seems to know more than it lets on. "I've got your back, Lara. Always." His words are simple, but they resonate within me, echoing through the caverns of doubt that had been hollowed out by my own insecurities.

The connection between us isn't just rekindled; it's as if we've struck a match to something richer, more enduring. It's trust, fortified and unwavering, and I bask in its warmth. This man has seen me at my worst, yet here he stands, offering not just his forgiveness, but also his support, without a second thought.

"And I've got yours," I say, feeling a glimmer of hope flicker to life. It's a fragile thing, this budding possibility of what could be between us, but it's there, and I hold onto it. With Jamie's compassion as my anchor, I let myself believe in the potential of a new beginning, one where the mistakes don't define us, but the way we rise above them does.

"Let's go get some ice cream," Jamie suggests, his casual tone laced with an undercurrent of something more, a promise, perhaps, of sweeter things to come.

"Sounds perfect," I reply, our shared laughter ringing clear and bright as we start walking side-by-side toward the exit.

The clinic door closes with a soft click behind us, and the cool evening air wraps around me like a gentle reminder that the world keeps turning. Our footsteps echo on the pavement, Jamie's steady pace matching mine as we head toward his car. The bandage around my finger feels snug, secure—much like the sense of camaraderie between us. I glance at him, trying to etch this moment of easy friendship into my memory, to treasure it when days are less kind.

"Thanks again for playing nurse," I murmur.

"Of course," Jamie responds, his voice low and reassuring. "It's the least I can do after you've seen so well to my injuries."

His words should be enough, they should fill the spaces inside me that doubt and uncertainty have carved out over time. And they do, mostly. But there's a flicker of something else, something wild and unpredictable that flares up unbidden. Wes's face, smirking and confident, flashes across my mind, and with it, the memory of his lips pressed against mine, insistent and fiery.

I bite my lip, attempting to push away the unwanted intrusion. It was just a kiss, a lapse in judgment that meant nothing. At least, that's what I keep telling myself, what I've assured Jamie of more times than I care to count. So why does the thought of it send my heart racing, my skin tingling with an awareness that refuses to be tamed?

We reach his car, and he opens the door to let me inside. As Jamie starts the engine, the soft hum of the dashboard lights offers a reprieve from the chaos of my thoughts. But even as I sit beside him, grateful for his presence, I can't shake the image of Wes from my mind. His touch lingers like a shadow, challenging the calm resolve I've built up around Jamie's kindness.

"So are you a chocolate person or a vanilla person?" asks Jamie, pulling out of the parking lot, unaware of the turmoil churning inside me.

"I'm a brownie batter person," I reply, forcing cheerfulness into my voice.

"Brownie batter it is!" he announces.

I try my best to be in the moment with my friend, the only friend I have on this team. But as the distance between the clinic and us grows, so does my confusion. Why does a kiss that supposedly meant nothing haunt my every quiet moment? Why does Wes's ghost trail my every step, taunting me with what-ifs and might-have-beens? I stare out the window at the passing streetlights, their glow blurring into streaks of gold against the night sky, and I wonder if I'll ever truly escape the heat of that reckless moment, or if it's seared itself onto my soul, indelible and undeniable.

CHAPTER TEN

The cooler autumn air touches my skin as I push through the doors of the practice facility, a mental checklist scrolling through my head. Supplies, session plans, rehab progress charts. I left them here in my rush yesterday, too caught up in my thoughts about Jamie and our date. We'd gone for ice cream, his treat, and he'd listened intently to every word I said, his eyes reflecting the warm glow of the setting sun.

He's perfect, I remind myself, the image of his smile lingering like the sweet aftertaste of brownie batter on my tongue. I feel like this is the way good relationships are supposed to go. Friends first, admirers. Then, later, when the time is right, lovers. That makes so much sense.

As I step into the cool interior, the echo of laughter pulls my attention away from my musings. The sound is infectious, bubbling with joy and youthful excitement, and it resonates from the direction of the ice rink. It's not what I expect on a quiet Saturday when the facility is typically deserted, save for a few dedicated athletes and their coaches.

Driven by an inquisitive pull, I veer off course, following the sound until I reach the rink's entrance. The chill from the ice seeps through the soles of my sneakers, but what freezes me in place isn't the temperature—it's the sight that unfolds before me.

Wes Carter stands at the center of a group of kids, each one hanging onto a hockey stick they can barely handle. They're a mismatched assembly, wearing donated gear that's seen better days. And there's Wes, guiding them with a patience I never knew he possessed, demonstrating a move with fluid grace that contradicts his usual brash swagger on the ice.

"Keep your knees bent, just like this," he instructs, bending his own to illustrate the point. "You'll have better balance that way."

I'm rooted to the spot, watching as he moves among them, offering words of encouragement or a helping hand to steady a wavering child. The kids are completely enamored, their gazes fixed on him with unbridled admiration. I feel something unfamiliar flutter in my chest, a warmth that has nothing to do with my affection for Jamie.

This is Wes? The same guy who's always armed with a comeback, whose presence in a room is akin to a storm brewing on the horizon? Now he's here, his eyes softening whenever one of the kids manages a wobbly lap around the cones he's set up.

"Good job, Marcus! You're getting the hang of it," Wes calls out, and the little boy beams, puffed up with pride.

There's a tenderness in his voice that catches me off guard, that doesn't fit with the image of the man I've pegged as nothing more than a charming troublemaker. I lean against the wall, arms crossed, unable to tear my gaze away from the scene. A part of me wonders why he's doing this, what compelled him to spend his morning teaching these kids.

And then it hits me—he's not just showing them how to play hockey. He's giving them something to believe in, a moment where they can feel like champions, regardless of the challenges they might face outside this rink. As I witness the genuine care he exhibits, my perception of Wes Carter begins to fracture, revealing glimpses of someone I haven't seen before.

A question buzzes in my mind, insistent and unbidden: If Jamie is perfect for me, why can't I shake off this sudden intrigue for Wes?

The last of the kids scatter from the rink, their laughter echoing off into the distance, leaving a strange quiet in its wake. I push off from the wall, my sneakers squeaking softly against the slick floor as I stride toward Wes. He's hunched over, gathering stray pucks into a bin, but he straightens up when he sees me approaching.

"Didn't peg you for a babysitter," I say before I can think better of it.

Wes's head tilts back, and that trademark grin lights up his face. "Well, I'm full of surprises, aren't I?" His smile morphs into something cheeky, eyes twinkling with mischief. "What about you? Playing hooky from work to spy on me?"

I roll my eyes but can't quite suppress a smile. "Just retrieving some equipment I left behind."

"Ah, so not stalking me then. I'm almost disappointed." He winks, and I feel an unexpected flutter in my stomach. I dismiss it with a shake of my head.

"Hardly," I retort, though my voice lacks conviction.

"Sure," he says, closing the distance between us until he's leaning closer, close enough that I can see flecks of gold in his hazel eyes. "So what did you think?"

"About what?" I feign ignorance, but I'm acutely aware of him—his height, the breadth of his shoulders, the unexpected gentleness I just witnessed.

"About the ice show," he says, motioning toward the now-empty rink. "You were watching for a while. I look good, don't I?"

He did. More than good. He's hard to look away from when he's in his element, dark hair tousled, wearing his casual jeans and a T-shirt that bares his tattoos.

I shrug, trying to appear nonchalant. "It was… nice to see you doing something good for those kids."

"Nice, huh?" His voice softens, and for a moment, the cocksure facade slips, revealing something earnest. "Those kids remind me of myself at their age. Hockey was my escape, you know? Gave me a purpose when things got rough at home."

The confession catches me off guard. Wes Carter, sharing a piece of his past without any bravado? It feels like a door creaking open, offering a glimpse inside a room I hadn't known existed.

"Is that why you do this?" I ask, motioning to the scattered hockey sticks and pucks around us.

"Partly," he admits, sitting down on the bench. "I guess I want to give them a chance at something better, even if it's just for an afternoon."

"Sounds like you've got more heart than I gave you credit for," I say quietly, joining him on the bench.

"Everyone has layers, Lara. Even me." Wes looks over at me, his gaze intense. It's disarming, seeing him like this—stripped of arrogance, human.

"Guess we're both full of surprises," I whisper, my mind flashing back to my own childhood—the rush of adrenaline on the track, the crushing despair when my leg gave out, and the dreams that crumbled with it.

"Tell me about it," Wes says, leaning in. "Your turn. What got you into sports therapy?"

"Used to run track," I begin, my voice a mere thread of sound. "Had Olympic dreams and all that. But after an injury took me out, I decided to help others achieve what I couldn't."

"Must have been tough," he says, and there's a resonance in his voice—a shared understanding of lost dreams.

"Wasn't easy to let go," I admit, and I'm surprised by how much I want to tell him, this man who I've only ever argued with. "But I found a new way to be part of athletics. And it turns out, I'm pretty happy with it."

"Resilient," Wes murmurs, nodding with respect. "I get that."

Our conversation flows, ebbing and swelling with tales of victories and defeats, of resilience and reinvention. We're no longer adversaries here; we're two kindred spirits sharing the broken road we've traveled. And as I listen to Wes speak, I realize there's a depth to him I'd never bothered to look for.

Maybe, just maybe, Wes Carter is more than the sum of the rumors that follow him. Maybe he's someone worth knowing, truly knowing. And as that thought takes root, I can't help but wonder what else lies beneath the surface of Wild Wes Carter.

And I shouldn't. He's the jerk who got the entire team thinking we have something going on when we don't.

We won't.

Which means I need to leave. Now.

Or, now.

But I can't. The more we talk, the more I want to talk to him. Eventually, the conversation winds down, and we part ways, the air forming a barrier between us once again. But the warmth lingers, a reminder of the connection we've shared.

I think of him all the while I'm collecting my things and straightening the PT room. I'm still thinking of him as I step outside, the late afternoon sun casting long shadows on the pavement, and I'm left grappling with a tangle of emotions.

Jamie is everything I thought I wanted—stable, kind, the perfect guy. Yet, as I walk to my car, Wes Carter invades my thoughts, challenging all my preconceived notions. Why am I so intrigued by the complexities of a man who's supposed to be my adversary?

Stop it, Lara, I scold myself, but my heart doesn't seem to be listening. Wes's passion, his unexpected tenderness with the kids, has sparked something in me. And as much as I want to dismiss it, to focus on the comfort Jamie offers, I can't shake the feeling that there's something about Wes that might just be worth exploring.

As the practice facility fades behind me, I'm left with a quiet disquiet, a question that refuses to be silenced: Why, if Jamie is perfect for me, can I not get Wes out of my head?

CHAPTER ELEVEN

The dimmed lights in the therapy room cast a gentle glow over Jamie's shoulder as I press down carefully, testing the mobility. It's late, way past the time when the last echoes of bouncing basketballs and screeching sneakers have faded from the gymnasium halls. The clock ticks a soothing rhythm that blends with our breaths.

"Ouch." Jamie winces, but his eyes are laughing. "I swear you find joy in my pain."

"Only the therapeutic kind," I retort, easing up on the pressure. My fingers probe the tender muscles, searching for knots and tension. "You wouldn't want your shoulder to freeze up on you, would you?"

"Guess I'm at your mercy then." His grin is boyish, charming in a way that makes my heart do somersaults.

"Always," I say, and there's more truth in that quip than I'd like to admit.

As I work the kinks out of Jamie's shoulder, I can't help but let my mind wander. Wes's image flashes before me—the bad boy of the team, with his reckless energy and unruly charm. And yet he was playing with those kids so naturally, as if he was genuinely having a great time with them. He's fire and ice, pushing everyone away, yet pulling them in just the same.

"Thinking hard?" Jamie's voice pulls me back, and I realize I've been silent for too long.

"Sometimes too much," I confess, forcing a smile. I don't want to speak Wes's name when I'm with Jamie, but I tell myself it's purely innocent curiosity, nothing he should mind. "Wes came by earlier, actually. He was… different. Not the usual storm cloud."

"Really?" Jamie sounds genuinely curious, and I nod.

"He stayed after practice to help clean up. Didn't say much, just did it." My hands pause as I remember the unexpected moment. "He has these rare instances of quiet kindness. Like he forgot to be mad at the world for a second. It makes me suspicious. Like he has something up his sleeve."

"Probably," Jamie murmurs, thoughtful. "He's all about himself."

"I don't think so. Sure, he might seem that way." I resume the massage, pressing into Jamie's muscle with renewed focus. "But there's dedication there, under all that brooding. To the game, to the team—even if he pretends otherwise."

"It's cutting through those layers of thorns," Jamie says softly. "I don't know if it's worth it."

"Have you tried?" I ask without thinking, glancing up to meet his gaze.

"Of course," he replies, a depth to his tone that hints at uncharted waters beneath his calm surface. "He doesn't let anyone get too close. He keeps his distance from all of us."

But he didn't keep his distance from me. He let me in on a small part of his life, and for a flicker, I feel special. The room feels smaller suddenly, the air charged with something fragile and unsaid. Jamie's presence is warm and grounding; it steadies the tremor that Wes's unpredictability sets off in me. One man like the eye of a storm, the other its unpredictable edge. Caught between them, I find myself adrift, wondering which way the wind will blow.

Jamie shifts, and I ease the pressure on his shoulder, watching as his brows knit. "You see something in him, don't you? In Wes?" His voice is a mixture of curiosity and something else—something like concern or maybe even jealousy. It's hard to read, especially with the way my own heart is tangled up.

"No, of course not," I admit with a sigh, looking down at my hands, which are now idle on Jamie's strong shoulder. "I guess it just intrigues me when a guy is so secretive. I have to wonder what he's hiding."

"I think he might just want us all to think he's got depth, when he's just a moody, cocky bastard," he responds, his fingers gently nudging my chin, prompting me to look at him. There's an openness in his face that urges honesty, makes me want to delve into things better left unsaid. But this is Jamie—good guy Jamie—who's always seen me, not the athlete or therapist, just Lara.

"Sometimes I think I can help him see the error of his ways, change him somehow so that he works better with the rest of the team." The words spill out before I can stop them, carrying with them a weight of responsibility I didn't realize I'd been shouldering. "But then I'm reminded that some people don't want to be saved, or they need to save themselves."

"True," Jamie agrees, his touch light and reassuring. "It's in your nature to help people, right? Just be careful, okay? People like Wes can pull you into their chaos before you know it."

"Is that what you think I'm doing? Getting pulled in?" The question hangs between us, fraught with implications about my feelings for both men.

"Maybe." He echoes my earlier response, his gaze searching mine. "But I trust you. You're the strongest person I know. And if you want to keep things professional, I'm sure you will."

My heart skips, warmth spreading through my chest at his words. Impulsively, I reach out, letting my fingers trace the line of his jaw. "Tell me something," I say, changing gears, needing to lighten the mood. "What's something no one else knows about Jamie Duncan?"

He chuckles, a sound that seems to vibrate through the room. "Well, for starters, I'm terrified of needles. Irony, right? A hockey player who can take a hit but can't handle a tiny jab."

Laughter bubbles up inside me, the tension of the moment easing. "Your secret's safe with me," I promise, feeling a connection to Jamie that goes beyond anything physical. It's genuine and deep, and for a fleeting second, I let myself bask in its glow.

Then, once again, my thoughts are pulled to Wes. He's *not* afraid of needles, judging from all those tattoos.

Stop it, Lara.

"Your turn," he says softly, the intensity back in his eyes. "Share something with me, Lara."

"Okay," I begin, my pulse quickening under his attentive gaze. "I still dream about running sometimes. Not about winning or competing, but just… running. Feeling the wind, the speed, the freedom. It's like flying, and when I wake up, for a moment, I forget I can't do it anymore."

"Sounds nice," he says, his voice barely above a whisper, our faces inches apart. His eyes hold mine, and there's a longing in them that mirrors the ache in my own heart—an ache for dreams lost and the possibility of new ones found in each other's presence.

Heat flushes my cheeks as Jamie's breath fans across my skin, his gaze locked onto mine with an intensity that sends a shiver down my spine. Time seems to slow, the sterile scent of antiseptic fading into the background, replaced by the subtle hint of his cologne—a mix of cedar and citrus that feels like it's wrapping around me. I can feel every beat of my heart, each one pounding against my ribcage, demanding attention, demanding action.

"Jamie," I whisper, a tremor in my voice betraying the storm of emotions inside me.

His eyes storm over. "I get it. Professional?" he murmurs.

But this is too perfect, and I'm aware I might never get another moment where I feel this certain. And maybe, just maybe, if I kiss Jamie, it will be enough to flush Wes's kiss out of my head.

I shake my head, almost imperceptibly, surrendering to this moment. It's all the invitation he needs.

His lips find mine in a gentle collision, a stark contrast to the tumultuous feelings raging within us. The kiss is soft at first, cautious—as if we're both testing the waters of this new, uncharted territory between us. But the caution quickly melts away under the heat of our connection, and the kiss deepens, growing more insistent, more urgent. Our bodies lean into each other as if drawn by a magnetic force we're powerless to resist. My hands find their way to his chest, feeling the steady thrum of his heartbeat beneath my palms.

For a moment, there is nothing else—no therapy room, no late night, no complicated love triangle—just Jamie and me and the overwhelming sense of rightness that floods through my veins. I lose myself in the kiss, in the intensity of the connection that crackles like electricity between us.

As I step back from Jamie, reality crashes over me like a wave, cold and jarring. Thoughts of Wes surge forward, unbidden, his beautiful face and moments of unexpected tenderness flashing through my mind. Guilt gnaws at my stomach, tangling with the remnants of desire that still pulse through my body. Jamie's eyes search mine, filled with questions I'm not ready to answer.

I back away. "Please...please don't tell...if Coach finds out that I..."

Jamie looks into my eyes with concern. The tension hangs heavy in the air until, without warning, my foot catches on a rogue therapy ball left out from our earlier session. My balance falters, and I stumble backward, a startled yelp escaping my lips.

Jamie's reflexes kick in—he reaches out, steadying me, but it's too late to prevent the flail that has me grasping for anything to break my fall. Instead of the hard floor, my hands land on Jamie's shoulders, pulling him into my clumsy dance.

Laughter erupts from both of us, uncontrollable and infectious. It bubbles up from somewhere deep inside me, a release valve for the tension that had been building all evening. My laughter mingles with Jamie's, two melodies intertwining in a moment of pure, unadulterated relief.

"Smooth move, Bennett," he teases, eyes twinkling with mirth as he helps me regain my footing.

"Occupational hazard," I counter, still chuckling, grateful for the respite from the emotional whirlwind. For a fleeting second, the room is filled with nothing but our shared amusement, the echo of our laughter a temporary balm for my racing heart and conflicted soul.

Regaining my composure, I stand straight, cheeks flushed from the fall—and from something else entirely. Jamie's hands linger on my arms, light but grounding, and I'm acutely aware of the warmth radiating from his touch.

"Looks like you've discovered a new therapy exercise," Jamie quips, the corners of his mouth upturned in that heart-melting smile. "We'll call it the 'Love Tumble.' Patented by Lara Bennett."

I can't help but laugh again, the sound softer this time, infused with the remnants of our earlier connection. There's an ease to Jamie, a gentle humor that wraps around me like a comforting blanket. It's moments like these that draw me to him, that make me forget the tangled web of emotions just outside this room.

"Only if it's guaranteed to fix more than just shoulder injuries," I say, playing along. His laughter joins mine, a harmonious duet that fills the empty therapy room. For a moment, it's as if we're the only two people in the world—no Wes, no complications, just us.

"Guaranteed to heal the heart, too," he adds, winking at me. The playful glint in his eyes sends a ripple of joy through me, washing away the confusion that had been clouding my mind.

"Is that so?" I ask, my voice laced with a teasing tone of its own. I notice how close we still are, his face mere inches from mine, the memory of our kiss lingering like a promise between us.

"Absolutely," he replies, confidence etched into his handsome features. "But don't worry. This secret is just between us. As long as you want it to be, okay?"

His words hang in the air, charged with unspoken possibilities. There's a silent acknowledgment of the growing attraction we both feel. A part of me wants to explore that attraction, to see where this unexpected path might lead. Jamie's presence is reassuring, his sincerity evident in every word and gesture. For now, I let myself melt into the happiness he offers, allowing his light to chase away the shadows of doubt—at least temporarily.

CHAPTER TWELVE

I adjust the resistance band wrapped around T-Rex's leg, my eyes focused on the slight tremble in his muscles. "Good, now remember to keep your core engaged and push against the tension—just like that," I coach, pride swelling within me as I watch him execute the movement flawlessly. This is why I'm here, why after my own dreams crashed and burned, I've dedicated my life to guiding others through their recovery.

"Got it, Lara," he grunts, a bead of sweat rolling down his temple.

"Three more reps," I encourage, though my attention flickers as my phone vibrates. Sliding it from my pocket, I glimpse Pat's name lighting up the screen with an urgency that can't be ignored. The message reads: *Interviewer coming your way asking about team injuries. Handle it.*

"Take a minute to rest," I tell T-Rex before stepping away, tucking my hair into a tighter ponytail. Whatever Pat needs, it's part of the job—even if dealing with the press is my least favorite aspect.

"Are you Lara Bennett?" A voice cuts through the buzz of the gym, assertive and laden with intent.

Turning, I meet the gaze of the woman advancing toward me. I cringe. I'd hoped it was Cassidy from the *Sun Beacon.* She's about the only reporter I can tolerate since she's T-Rex's girlfriend and has a nice, soft touch. But this woman is clearly anything *but* soft. Her stance screams tenacity, her eyes sharp and calculating behind sleek frames. Sarah Thompson, the name tag clipped to her blazer announces.

"That's me," I reply, bracing myself for what's to come.

The reporter turns to her cameraman and makes sure he's in position before starting. "Sarah Thompson, *Daily Sports Watch.* I have a few questions about the recent injuries on the team," she says, but her eyes hold a different curiosity. "But first, there are rumors swirling about your relationship with Wes Carter. Can you comment on that?"

The question hits like a rogue wave, and I steady myself. How can anyone possibly know...did the players leak that gossip? And even if they did, what business is it of anyone else? "My relationship with all the players is strictly professional. I'm here to ensure they're in top physical condition."

"Of course." Sarah nods, her expression unchanging. "But there's talk of some… heated interactions with Wes Carter. He's quite the favorite, especially among the ladies, so of course, our listeners want to know. Anything you'd care to clarify for the fans?"

"Look, it's not true. As for Wes, we have a… complex working dynamic. That's all there is to it." I'm careful with my words, knowing how easily they can be twisted.

"Complex? How so?" she probes, her pen poised over her notepad like a predator ready to pounce.

"Let's just say that he's had some challenging injuries that we've had to work past," I deflect, feeling the weight of her scrutiny. "Now, if you have questions about the team's health, I'd be happy to discuss our rehabilitation programs."

Sarah purses her lips, evidently not satisfied, but she scribbles a note. "We'll circle back to that. For now, let's talk about those programs."

I shift in my seat, feeling the cushion's support beneath me as I redirect Sarah's attention to the heart of my work. "The team's success is a collective effort," I say with conviction. "Their resilience is remarkable, and it's an honor to facilitate their recovery."

Sarah leans in closer, her gaze sharp and questioning. "That's commendable, Lara. But the public is curious about more than just your professional achievements. They want to know about you—specifically, your personal connections."

Back to that. The muscles in my back tense, a familiar discomfort as I recognize the turn this conversation is taking. My responses become more clipped, my patience wearing thin. "My focus here is on the players' well-being. Their ability to return to the ice is what matters most." I stand, signaling that the interview has reached its natural conclusion.

"Of course," she says, rising with a smoothness that contradicts her relentlessness. "But surely—"

"Thank you for your time, Sarah," I interject, hoping my tone conveys the finality I'm desperate for. I'm really hoping most of this interview ends up on the cutting room floor after editing, because it's not exactly the kind of juicy headlines that will glue people to their screens. Is it? Then again, Wes is very controversial, a player, a man known for making headlines. Maybe his romantic entanglements *are* of interest to fans. "If there are no further questions about my work, I need to get back to my patients."

"Very well," she concedes, though the gleam in her eye tells me she's far from done.

Just as I feel the weight of the interview lifting, the door swings open and Wes strides in, his presence filling the room like a sudden storm. "Hey, Lara, tell the lovely reporter about our passionate fling," he calls out, his voice carrying an edge of mischief.

At that moment, it hits me like a thunderbolt. Was *he* the one who told reporters? Heat floods my cheeks as I turn to him, words stumbling over each other in their haste to correct his narrative. "Wes, that's not true," I manage, but the damage is done.

Sarah's eyes light up, her pen ready to record every syllable. "A fling, you say? How does this fit into the 'complex dynamic' you mentioned earlier?"

"Nothing fits because there's nothing going on," I say firmly, trying to recover the situation. "Wes enjoys making jokes in poor taste."

"Is that what it is? A joke?" Sarah's question hangs in the air like an accusation, and Wes winks at me, a silent challenge that sends my heart racing for all the wrong reasons.

Heart pounding, I shove the door closed behind me, craving sanctuary from the prying eyes and insinuating whispers.

I've only been in there for half an hour, organizing my workspace, when my phone buzzes against the wooden surface of my desk, a jarring intrusion into the quiet I so desperately need. It's Naomi. She doesn't text during work hours unless it's important—or scandalous.

I swipe to unlock my phone, and there it is: a link to the interview. The thumbnail alone—a shot of Wes with that signature smirk, his arm slung casually around an empty chair next to him—makes my stomach churn.

Have you seen this? her message reads, accompanied by three wide-eyed emojis.

The video starts playing, and it's even worse than I feared. Sarah's voice overlays clips of our confrontation, spinning a narrative of forbidden romance and secret rendezvous between team therapist and notorious bad boy. And apparently, the only parts that ended up on the cutting room floor are the ones where I denied the relationship and called Wes out on his joke. Each word twists the knife deeper, and I can't help but cringe at how out of context my defensive reactions look.

I shoot a text back to Naomi, my fingers fumbling in haste. *It's not true,* I write, punctuated with a frustrated sigh.

Sure, Lara. That's what they all say. But I'm sure no one will believe you fended off the advances of that hot piece of man flesh. Naomi's reply comes with a winking emoji, but I can tell she's worried for me.

I jab in the response.

Seriously, Nae. There's nothing going on between Wes and me.

Her response is instantaneous.

Ok, I believe you. But what about Jamie? Have you talked to him yet?

I wince. Jamie. He'll be hurt, and understandably. Only Naomi knows that I've been thinking anything about Wes at all, and I'd sworn her to secrecy. During our conversation, I'd been cautiously optimistic that Jamie and I were building slowly to something more.

But now, thanks to that news report...everyone will know exactly what is in my heart. It doesn't matter how much I try to deny it. It's true.

Her question hangs in virtual space, unanswered, as I drop my phone on the desk. Leaning back in my chair, I press my hands over my face, letting the coolness of my palms try to soothe the heat of embarrassment.

What am I going to tell Jamie? He already extended me the grace of trust once when I assured him my relationship with Wes was strictly professional. But now, with Wes's reckless claims hanging in the air like a toxic cloud, I'm not sure that trust will hold. Every glance, every casual touch between Wes and me, will be scrutinized, weighed for evidence of something more.

Jamie's image rises unbidden in my mind—those earnest blue eyes, the steadiness that anchors his every move. If he hears the rumors, fueled by Wes's ridiculous antics, could I blame him for doubting me?

And then there's the dangerous truth I keep locked away: the flicker of attraction to Wes that I've been trying to smother, a flame that threatens to ignite if fanned by his provocations. It's a game to him, but it's playing with fire for me. If I'm not careful, I'll get burned, and in the process, I might just drive Jamie away.

"Damn you, Wes," I whisper, the words a blend of anger and a plea. "What have you done?"

CHAPTER THIRTEEN

The crisp smell of ice and the sound of blades carving into it greet me as I push through the double doors into the training facility. My pulse quickens, a familiar thrill coursing through me, reminiscent of my sprinting days. Although that chapter of my life is closed, this new role as a sports therapist has allowed me to harness that energy in a different way. Today, there's an electric anticipation hanging over the rink; the next game is pivotal, and every player knows it.

I weave through the bustle, exchanging nods with staff and players alike. The crack of sticks against pucks forms a rhythm that syncs with my heartbeat. I'm here to ensure these athletes stay at their peak, but watching them glide across the ice, so focused and determined, I can't help but feel a part of something greater—like each stride on the ice pulses through me too.

The swing of the side door catches my attention, drawing eyes from all corners of the rink. She steps in, as if on cue for some unwritten dramatic entrance—a cascade of glossy hair, a smile that lights up the room, and a walk that somehow combines grace and confidence in a way that seems effortless.

"Veronica," someone breathes out, almost reverently.

The atmosphere shifts palpably, as though someone turned up the brightness just a notch. The players, mid-practice, slow down, catching sight of her one by one. Even from here, I can see why she commands such attention. Veronica is stunning, the kind of beauty that doesn't need the spotlight because it follows her anyway.

"Hey, guys," she calls out, voice melodic yet strong enough to carry over the icy expanse. "I just couldn't stay away. Missed watching you all in action."

"Missed you more," comes a chorus of replies, each laced with varying degrees of warmth and cheerfulness.

I stand there, observing, feeling a small twist in my gut that I quickly label as professional concern. They should be focusing on practice, not... But who am I kidding? A twinge of jealousy tugs at me—not for the attention they give her, but for the camaraderie she shares with them, a camaraderie I'm still on the outskirts of. It's silly, really, but there it is, niggling at the back of my mind.

She laughs, and it's like a melody that hooks everyone in. I watch them all, these giants on blades, turn into boys eager for just a glance from her. And they get it, her gaze flitting over each face, leaving smiles in its wake. I adjust the strap of my medical bag, suddenly very aware of the practical clothing hugging my athletic frame—so starkly utilitarian next to her effortlessly chic attire.

"Practice hard, boys," she says with a wink, and they all nod, seemingly spurred on by her presence.

"Will do, V!" one of the players shouts back, enthusiasm spiking.

"Always do when you're around," another adds with a grin.

The practice resumes, intensity dialed up a notch, as if her mere presence has infused them with something extra. I shake off the strange mix of emotions and refocus on my purpose here. My job is to keep them healthy, to ensure their bodies can sustain the drive and passion they pour onto the ice.

"Okay, Bennett," I mutter under my breath, "let's get to work."

Before I can, though, I hear the sharp sound of heels clicking toward me on the cement. The coolness of the ice rink contrasts sharply with the heat that flushes my cheeks as Veronica strides toward me. The swish of her skirt seems to keep time with the thudding of my heart, each step a melodramatic beat leading to an inevitable crescendo.

"Hey," she says, brushing a loose strand of hair from her face, her smile practiced but not reaching her eyes. "You're the new physical therapist, Lara, right?"

I nod, my response caught somewhere between a greeting and an affirmation. "That's me. And you are…?"

"Veronica Wilkes. I'm Wes's ex-girlfriend. But still a friend of the team." Her perfectly arched eyebrow rises just a fraction, but it may as well be a red flag billowing in warning. "I saw your interview," she continues, the smooth timbre of her voice now edged with something sharp. "Wes seemed quite taken with you."

I feel the weight of the players' stares, their curious glances bouncing between us like a silent rally. "Oh, that," I stammer, trying to downplay the tension coiling in the air. "It was just a joke."

"Was it?" Her laugh is hollow, a ghost of the melody it was moments ago. "I dated Wes for seven years, Lara. I think I know when he's joking. That wasn't it."

The words hang heavy, and suddenly the rink feels smaller, the walls creeping inward. A collective intake of breath from the players fills the void left by our halted conversation—a symphony of shock that only amplifies the silence that follows. I can almost hear the click of mental gears as they piece together implications and past histories.

My mouth is dry; I taste the bitter tang of embarrassment as I try to salvage the situation. This is not the stage on which I wanted to play out my professional life. But here I am, center ice, under the scrutiny of an audience I'm not ready to face.

"I—Veronica," I begin, but the words clump together like wet snow. "Professional boundaries are something I take very seriously. Wes and I, we have a working relationship, nothing more."

But even as I speak, I can feel the doubt blooming around me, fed by the skepticism in Veronica's gaze and nurtured by the whispers that start to ripple through the ranks of the players. My confidence wanes, and I struggle to appear unaffected, to maintain the composed facade I've worked so hard to build.

"Of course," she replies, her tone dripping with unspoken meaning. "Just looking out for a… friend."

I nod once, curtly, wishing the ground would open up beneath me or, at the very least, that I could melt away like ice under a spring sun. Instead, I stand there, exposed and vulnerable, grappling with professionalism and the raw sting of public exposure. The silence stretches, suffocating. I draw in a deep breath, willing my heart rate to slow, my cheeks to cool. But it's as if the air itself is conspiring against me, thick with tension and unspoken questions.

My gaze darts around, seeking an ally, landing on Jamie. He's been unusually silent, his expression unreadable. Then, without a word, he pushes off the ice, skates cutting a sharp path away from center ice, toward the locker room. My stomach drops; even Jamie won't meet my eyes.

"Jamie—" My voice trails off as I watch him disappear into the locker room. I'm left grappling with the realization that this isn't just about me and Veronica anymore. It's about the team, their trust, and the fragile line I walk between personal and professional.

"Guess practice is over for some of us," someone quips, but the levity is gone. I can't help but feel responsible for the shift in atmosphere, for the fractures forming in relationships I'm still learning to navigate.

The door swings shut behind Veronica with a finality that echoes in the empty space she leaves behind. I gather the remnants of my composure, smoothing down my ponytail, a nervous gesture I thought I had outgrown. I need to talk to Jamie to explain—something, anything, that might bridge the distance I sense growing between us.

I make my way toward the locker room, my resolve firming with each step. But when I reach the door, Jamie emerges, his face set, a storm brewing in those eyes I've come to admire.

"Jamie, can we talk?" I ask, my voice steadier than I feel.

"Not right now, Lara." His voice is terse, clipped with an edge I'm not accustomed to. "I've got to go."

And then he's brushing past me, leaving nothing but a swirl of cold air and a knot of worry settling deep in my gut. "You don't actually believe what that reporter said on the—"

He swings around suddenly, startling me. "No. I didn't believe her. That's why I never brought it up to you. But Veronica tells you that Wes has the hots for you, and what did you do? You didn't tell her the feeling wasn't mutual. No, I saw it in your face. If it walks like a duck…what the hell am I supposed to believe, Lara?"

He turns and jogs toward the back of the locker room, pulling his jersey up over his head before disappearing in a cloud of steam. I watch his retreating figure, fighting the urge to call after him, to fix whatever this is before it grows too large to mend.

I stand in the stillness of the training facility, my heart thumping against my ribs like a trapped bird. The air feels heavier now, charged with a tension that seems to seep into the very walls. I can almost hear the whispered exchanges around me, feel the weight of curious glances that don't quite meet my eyes.

It's as if Veronica's words have left a residue, a thin film of doubt and speculation that clings to everything she touched. My own thoughts are a jumble, tripping over each other in their haste to make sense of it all. It's unsettling how quickly the camaraderie of the morning has dissolved, replaced by this uncomfortable silence.

I need to clear the air. And there's only one person who can help me with that.

I about-face and head back to the rink. Once filled with the sharp scrapes of skates and the slap of pucks, it now holds only the ghost of action. Even the scent of cold ice seems smothered by the awkwardness that blankets us. Players shuffle out, their usual boisterous laughter subdued, their playful banter muted to murmurs and half-hearted chuckles.

I catch sight of Wes across the ice, his eyes alight with something unreadable as he watches me. I look away, not ready to decipher his expression or confront the smug tilt of his lips. I'm used to being on solid ground, knowing my role, my purpose. But today, that certainty is stripped from me, leaving a vulnerability I can't afford to show.

"Rough day, huh?" Lawson's voice slices through my reverie, her tone softer than I expect.

"Something like that," I admit, unable to mask the strain in my voice.

I expect her to read me the riot act on professionalism, especially in the wake of the media shitstorm Wes caused. But as she fixes me with her piercing gaze, a silent message passes between us. There's an unspoken understanding, maybe even respect, in her scrutiny. She may question my methods, but we both know the sting of being judged in a male-dominated world.

"Shake it off, Bennett. You've got work to do," she says firmly, before turning on her heel and marching toward her office.

The coach's presence is a stark reminder of why I'm here. Not for love. To work. It's a mistake to talk to Wes, to feed the drama monster. That's what he wants—to raise eyebrows. And I'm just playing into his hands.

What I need to do is create distance. Coach is right. I need to shake it off and get back to what really matters.

"Right," I murmur to myself, her words grounding me for a moment. But as the sound of her retreating footsteps fades, I'm left alone amidst the echoes of a day I'd rather forget. My hands find my hips, and I take a deep breath, trying to dislodge the tightness in my chest.

I need to regroup, to refocus on why I'm here. These athletes rely on me to be at my best, despite whatever personal drama unfolds. I refuse to let Wes—or anyone—derail me from my path.

CHAPTER FOURTEEN

The bass thrums through my body, a pulsating heartbeat that mirrors the vibrancy of the bar. Laughter spills from every corner, mingling with the scent of spiced rum and citrus. It's one of those nights where the energy is palpable, and Naomi and I are at the center of it all, clinking glasses in a toast to unwinding after a week that tested the limits of our patience.

"Here's to finally having a break," Naomi yells over the music, her eyes twinkling with mischief.

I nod, sipping my drink—a mix of tart and sweet that sets my taste buds alight. This is what freedom feels like, shedding the constraints of work and letting loose.

"So…about Jamie…" she goes on.

I shake my head. I don't want to talk about him. He thinks I'm hung up on Wes, and I might have been. But not now. Now, I'm a free agent. "Let's find a couple of hot guys and have some fun. Ones that don't play hockey. Deal?"

She grins. "Deal."

But that thought goes by the wayside as I scan the crowd, and a new sensation prickles across my skin.

He's here.

Wes Carter strides into the bar like he owns the place, and maybe he does—in spirit, at least. Confidence rolls off him in waves, his leather jacket hugging his shoulders like a second skin. It's hard not to stare; he has this magnetic pull that demands attention, and my gaze lingers longer than I intend.

"Damn," I groan under my breath.

"Look who decided to grace us with his presence," Naomi says, following my eyes to where Wes leans against the bar, ordering a drink with that easy smile that seems permanently etched onto his face.

His nickname suits him perfectly. There's something untamed about him, from the tousled dark hair that falls just over his brow to the way his jeans cling to his legs, hinting at the strength beneath.

"Keep your distance, Lara," I mutter under my breath, turning away.

"Hey, sprinter!" Wes calls out, and I flinch, caught off guard by the nickname that harkens back to my college days. His voice weaves through the noise, finding me with pinpoint accuracy.

"Hey yourself," I reply, injecting a nonchalance I don't feel. My pulse quickens as he saunters over, that cocky grin growing as he closes the distance between us.

"Didn't take you for a barfly, Bennett," he teases, leaning closer so I can hear him over the music. The proximity sends a jolt through me, a bolt of electricity that sings in my veins.

"Couldn't say the same about you, Mr. Hangover," I shoot back, but it lacks bite. Damn him for being so effortlessly charming.

"Ah, but I blend in with the nightlife—it's my natural habitat." Wes's voice dips lower, intimate, and my heart skips a beat. "I'm kidding, really. I don't drink all that much. You just caught me at my worst. I'm dealing with some stuff…"

I blink, shocked that he's revealing something personal and not going for the pick-up line. "Like what?"

He shakes it off. "Nothing. But I wanted to thank you for not telling Lawson when you found me like that. She probably would've lost it."

This is not a good recipe. Alcohol, combined with gorgeous Wes, expressing a rare moment of appreciation. I'm in danger of falling for him. So I steel myself. "I had the mind to."

"But you didn't," he points out, grinning. "And now you're here, and I'm sure Lawson wouldn't be happy to see her PT letting loose the night before a big game. What's your excuse?"

"Recovering from a long week," I answer truthfully, trying to ignore the way his gaze seems to pierce right through me.

"And I thought it was fate, bringing us together," he says, a suggestive edge to his words. "How about a dance?"

"Thanks, but I should—" I start, thinking of Jamie's expression when he last spoke to me, but Wes cuts me off with a tilt of his head.

"Come on, one dance won't hurt." His hand brushes mine, sending unexpected warmth spiraling up my arm.

"I don't think so," I protest weakly, but even as I say it, I'm aware of how hollow it sounds.

"Coach isn't here, Lara. I am." It's like he can read my mind. Wes's voice is soft, almost tender, and it's enough to make me waver. I'm drawn into his orbit, fighting the gravity of his presence.

“Maybe later,” I mumble.

He simply shrugs and walks away, only to be swallowed by a sea of willing females.

Jealousy pulses through me. Why do I wish I was one of them?

Gulping down the last of my drink, I twist a strand of hair around my finger—an anxious habit. Naomi leans against the bar, her eyes flitting between Wes and me with an all-knowing glint.

“Sparks were flying there, Lara,” she murmurs, nudging me with her elbow. “You could cut the tension with a knife.”

I let out a shaky breath, feeling the weight of her observation settle in my gut. “I don’t know what you’re talking about,” I lie, but my voice betrays me, cracking under the strain of concealed truths.

“Come on, it’s me,” Naomi says, turning to face me fully, her expression earnest. “You’ve got that look in your eye, the same one you had when you were gearing up for a big race. Except now, I think you’re running toward something—or someone—instead of away. You should dance with him. Let loose. You wanted to meet a hot guy…you can’t possibly find anyone hotter than Wild Wes Carter. And I know you like him.”

The comparison strikes a chord, stirring the dormant competitor within me. My gaze drifts back to Wes, who’s engaged in conversation with a group of women, yet his attention flickers to me occasionally, like a lighthouse beacon guiding ships home.

“I don’t know. I messed things up with Jamie, and I need to repair it,” I start hesitantly, my conflict rising like a tide. “Talking to Wes feels like making things worse. He’s like a storm. Exciting, unpredictable, and I’m inexplicably drawn to him.”

“Is it just the thrill, or is there something more?” Naomi probes gently, her concern evident.

I chew on my bottom lip, considering her question. Jamie’s an open book. With him, what you see is what you get. Wes always reveals tiny bits of himself, just enough to make me yearn to know more. “It’s not just the excitement. When Wes looks at me, it’s as if he sees something no one else does. It’s like he’s leaving threads for me, and only me, inviting me to pull them. It’s intense and… seductive.”

Naomi’s brow furrows, her lips pressed into a thin line. “Be careful, Lara. Bad boys like Wes often leave a trail of heartache. You might enjoy the chase now, but what happens when the game ends?”

I wince, knowing her warning comes from a place of love. “He’s not just a bad boy, Naomi. He had a long-term girlfriend. And there are moments when he's… sweet. Like he genuinely cares. There's something behind the façade. I just need to chip away at it." I pause, the words tasting bitter on my tongue. "But then there's Jamie, who's sweet all the time, without fail."

"Sounds like you're in between a rock and a hard place," she comments dryly.

"Exactly," I admit. "With Jamie, it's friendship, slow and steady. The kind you build a life on. But with Wes, it's this thrilling but uncertain connection that makes me feel alive in ways I can't explain."

"Life's not a sprint, Lara. It's a marathon," Naomi says softly, placing a supportive hand on my shoulder. "Whichever path you choose, make sure it's one you can run on for the long haul."

Her advice echoes in my ears, a stark reminder of the choice looming ahead. Jamie represents the finish line I always envisioned, while Wes is the unexpected hurdle that could change my course forever.

I groan into my empty glass. "I don't know. I should tell both of them to get lost. I need to stay professional. At least until I get my contract renewed. It's just so…hard."

"I'd find it hard, too, with those two hotties around," she says, licking her lips. "Why don't you choose one and leave the other one for me?"

I give her a look.

The rhythm of the bar pulses through me, a beat that's fast and fierce like the races I used to run. My heart syncs with it as Naomi leans in, her voice a soft contrast to the cacophony around us. "Just remember what matters to you, Lara. What are your priorities? Think about what could happen if you get swept up in a whirlwind with Wes."

"Priorities," I murmur, tasting the word. It feels heavy on my tongue, laden with responsibility. My job was always my priority. But what about my happiness? Isn't that the overall goal?

Naomi is right; I've always been someone who looks ahead, calculating each step before I take it. Until now. With Wes, it's like I'm learning to walk again—stumbling, unsure.

"Emotions that swing back and forth can be… exhilarating," she continues, her gaze steady, "but they can also leave you unbalanced. You thrive on stability, on knowing where you stand. That's important for the long-term, isn't it?"

I nod slowly, feeling a familiar ache in my knee—a ghost pain from an old injury and a reminder of a past where every decision was about the long game. "You're right," I concede, but my agreement is hollow. The thought of not exploring this electric connection with Wes makes my chest tighten.

Before I can drown further in my own conflicted thoughts, he's there, materializing from the throng like a phantom made flesh. "Lara," Wes says, and his voice is a smooth caress, "I have to call it a night in a bit. Need to get my beauty sleep for tomorrow. So how about that dance? Something innocent to cap off the night."

Innocent. The word doesn't seem to fit in the same sentence as Wes, and yet, I find myself nodding, drawn to him like a moth to flame. His hand is warm around mine, guiding me through the crowd to an open space where bodies sway and collide in rhythmic chaos.

As soon as we start moving to the music, I'm enveloped by his presence. The heat from his body, the firmness of his hands on my hips, it's overwhelming, intoxicating. He draws me closer, and I let him, lost in the moment, the thumping bassline a backdrop to my racing heart.

"See? Nothing but a simple dance," Wes murmurs against my ear, his breath hot on my skin.

Simple. Right. There's nothing simple about the way my body responds to his touch, about the way my mind reels with the possibilities of what this dance could lead to. I can feel the tension coiling tighter within me, threatening to snap.

"Too close," I whisper, more to myself than to him. The realization crashes over me like a wave—I'm out of control, and it terrifies me. I'm not one to relinquish control, not since the days when control meant everything on the track.

With a surge of willpower that leaves my limbs trembling, I lean back. Wes's eyes search mine, a flicker of something unreadable passing through them. "I need to think," I say, as much an apology as an explanation.

He nods, a graceful acceptance that's at odds with the predatory charm I've come to associate with him. "Fine."

He lets me go, as simple as that. The instant his arms loosen, I want them to tighten again. Hating myself for that, I turn away, my pulse still racing, but now out of fear rather than desire. Fear of making the wrong choice, fear of losing what I have with Jamie, fear of the unknown that Wes represents. I have to sort this out, figure out which finish line I'm running toward before I commit to the race.

The cool night air hits me as Naomi and I step out of the bar, a stark contrast to the warmth and noise we leave behind. I breathe hard, my breath dissipating like the remnants of the tension I'm trying so hard to shake off. Beside me, Naomi's heels click rhythmically against the pavement, an orderly beat that seems to mock the disarray of my emotions.

"Are you okay?" Naomi asks, her voice laced with concern that slices through the fog of my thoughts.

I give her a half-smile, nodding. "Yeah, just… thinking." My words trail off into the night.

We walk side by side in silence, the earlier conversation about Wes's uneven emotions echoing in my mind. Naomi's right; I know she is. But logic doesn't seem to hold much weight against the pull I feel toward him, the magnetic force that drew me into his orbit despite my best intentions.

A part of me—a reckless, daring part—wishes I'd allowed myself one more moment of weakness, one more kiss to savor and regret. *It's foolish,* I scold myself. *You're not a girl who acts on every impulsive desire, Lara Bennett. You're someone who knows the importance of control, discipline, and making choices with clear intentions.*

But as we round the corner onto the quieter street where I live, a pang of sadness tightens around my heart. The vivid memory of Wes's lips on mine, that intoxicating first kiss, haunts me. The taste of possibility, so sweet and dangerous, tempts me with what-ifs and might-have-beens.

"Hey." Naomi gently bumps her shoulder against mine, pulling me from my reverie. "You look like you're a thousand miles away."

"Feels like it," I admit, forcing a chuckle that doesn't quite reach my eyes.

"Whatever you decide, I'm here for you," she says, sincerity shining in her gaze. "Just remember, there's more to life than chasing thrills. Sometimes the steady flame burns brightest, you know?"

I nod, appreciating her words even though they stir a fresh wave of confusion within me. Jamie is the steady flame, the unwavering light in my life. And then there's Wes, flickering and unpredictable, casting shadows and light in equal measure.

"Thanks, Naomi." My gratitude is genuine, but it does little to ease the ache in my chest or quiet the whisper of longing that says I should've taken the risk, should've kissed him again.

When we reach my apartment building, she gives me a hug. "Call me tomorrow," she tosses over her shoulder as she heads to her car.

“Will do.” I cast a glance back in the direction of the bar, half wondering if Wes is standing on the dance floor, thinking about me with that knowing smile of his.

Inside my apartment, I close the door, leaning back against the wood as I replay the evening in my head. The music, the laughter, the heat of Wes’s body against mine as we danced—it all blurs together into a mess of emotion I can’t untangle.

Jamie’s face swims into my mind, his kind eyes filled with a love that’s simple and true. And yet, the memory of Wes’s touch still lingers on my skin, igniting a fire that refuses to be extinguished.

I sink to the floor, wrapping my arms around my knees. The decision weighs heavy on me, a choice between the comfort of the familiar and the allure of the unknown.

I wish I had kissed him again, if only to prove to myself that I could resist him afterward. But wishes are as fleeting as a breeze in the night, and regret is a shadow that follows too closely.

For now, I need to sort through this tangle of feelings to understand the path my heart truly wants to take. Because whether it leads to Jamie or Wes, I refuse to run a race whose finish line I haven’t chosen for myself.

CHAPTER FIFTEEN

The sun dips low on the horizon as I trudge out of the practice facility, my body weighed down by the kind of fatigue that seeps into your bones. It's been a day of endless sessions of pushing athletes through pain and coaxing muscles back to life. Now, all I want is the solace of a hot shower and the comfort of my couch.

The past few weeks have been some of the most tiring of my life. I've been doing a dance of avoidance, helping the players, remaining detached. Thankfully, Jamie and Wes haven't needed my help, so I've been able to navigate the dangerous waters with relative ease. The only problem is…I have to admit, I miss them. I miss the way Wes's sexy smirk would get my heart pumping, the way Jamie's friendship and easy conversation always brightened my day.

It's better this way, I tell myself.

And it is. Pat Lawson hasn't gotten on my back over my "reckless" therapy practices or relationship rumors, and I'm grateful for that. The team's injuries as a whole have gone down. So that's all good news.

I reach my car, toss my bag into the back seat, and slide behind the wheel. I turn the key in the ignition, but the engine only groans—a pitiful, sputtering sound that sends a wave of frustration through me. Not now. I twist the key again, harder this time, as if my sheer will could jumpstart the stubborn vehicle. The car responds with silence.

"Come on," I mutter under my breath, banging a fist against the steering wheel. I pop the hood, step out, and stare at the engine as if it might reveal its secrets to me. It doesn't. Of course, it doesn't.

"Car trouble?"

The voice comes from behind me, low and tinged with a hint of amusement. I don't have to turn around to know who it is—Wes Carter, with his roguish looks and that insufferable smirk that seems permanently etched onto his face.

"Brilliant observation," I snap without looking at him, still scrutinizing the engine with unqualified eyes.

"Mind if I take a look?" he asks, already moving closer.

"Be my guest," I say, stepping aside with a huff. "Not like I'm making any progress."

Wes rolls up the sleeves of his worn practice jersey, revealing forearms lined with tattoos and the scars of a man who's no stranger to physical work. He leans in, his attention fixed on the guts of my car, hands moving with a confidence that's annoyingly attractive.

"Looks like you've got a dead battery," he says after a moment, his head popping back up. "Either that or the connections are loose. Happens sometimes."

"Great," I mutter. "Just what I needed today."

"Got jumper cables?" Wes asks, glancing over at me. His eyes hold mine for a second too long.

"Trunk," I reply, pointing vaguely toward the back of the car.

He retrieves them with ease and then pops open the hood of an old Mustang I hadn't even noticed parked next to me. I should feel relieved, thankful even, but there's a tension in my chest that has nothing to do with the car.

"Stand back," Wes instructs, setting up the cables. There's a spark as he connects them, and a part of me sparks too—against my better judgment.

"Red to red, black to black," he murmurs, mostly to himself. "Alright, try it now."

I slide back into the driver's seat, holding my breath as I turn the key once more. The engine roars to life, and a small victory flares inside me, quickly doused by the reality of who I owe it to.

"Thanks," I say grudgingly, not quite meeting his gaze as I emerge from the car.

"Anytime." Wes grins, disconnecting the cables. "You might want to get that checked out, though. Don't want you stranded somewhere less… convenient."

"Right," I say, nodding curtly.

There's an awkward pause, the cool air between us thickening even more with unspoken words and lingering glances. I break it first, because I need to get the last word in, always.

"Guess you're not just a pretty face and bad attitude."

"Who knew?" Wes chuckles, a warm sound that does strange things to my pulse.

"Definitely not me," I admit before I can stop myself.

The corners of his lips twitch upward, and it strikes me then—just how dangerous this game could be.

Wes leans against the hood of my car, his hands now free from their mechanical dance under the hood. The afternoon sun casts a golden hue on his face, softening the sharp lines that I've always associated with his cocksure grin and troublemaker's glint. There's a shift in his demeanor, an unfamiliar vulnerability that hangs awkwardly on him like a borrowed coat.

"Look, Lara," he starts, and there's something in his voice that pins me in place. "I know I haven't been… well, I haven't been the kind of guy you can rely on. I haven't been all that nice to you."

My arms cross over my chest protectively, as if they could shield me from whatever confession is coming. My heart picks up speed, but I keep my face impassive. "You're not wrong there," I reply, trying to maintain a lightness I don't feel.

He runs a hand through his hair—a nervous gesture that seems out of place on him. "I've been a jerk to you more than once. And it wasn't fair. Especially since I know you're trying to impress Coach." His gaze locks onto mine, insistent, pleading for understanding—or maybe forgiveness. "But, God help me, I can't stop thinking about you, Lara. These feelings have been eating at me."

The air between us crackles, charged with an intensity that feels both foreign and dangerously familiar. My throat tightens, skepticism warring with the part of me that wants to believe him. Wants to dive into the possibility of what these feelings might mean.

"Feelings?" The word tastes bitter on my tongue. "Which ones? Annoyance? Disdain?" I challenge, but my voice lacks the conviction I'm aiming for.

"No. The opposite, actually." He steps closer, his eyes earnest, searching. "I've got a thing for you, Lara. For real. And I'm sorry for all the crap before. I guess I wanted to know…if you felt the same?"

I recoil slightly, as if the words themselves could wound me. It's too much, too fast, and from Wes of all people—Wes, who has always been a storm I knew better than to get caught in. My mind is a whirlpool of confusion, every instinct telling me to run, while something deeper, something I thought I'd buried long ago, wonders if there could be truth in his eyes.

There's a tremor in my hands, hidden from view, betraying the chaos inside. No one has ever seen me as anything but the former athlete turned therapist, the girl who put her dreams aside to fix others'. But Wes—reckless, infuriating Wes—is looking at me like I'm more than just a conquest to him. Like I'm someone worth apologizing to. Worth having feelings for.

"I'll admit that I'm attracted to you," I say, not sure I should, because I can't help but wonder if it's something that will get me in trouble. "But so are a lot of women. You know that better than anyone. What I don't like is how you blow hot and cold all the time. You reveal just enough of yourself to get me curious, and then that bravado gets in the way. I never know what's real with you, and what's Wild Wes, playing games."

He winces. "Yeah. I'm sorry."

"Apologies are easy," I say, voice steady despite the storm inside. "Proving it? That's where things fall apart." My defenses are up, walls fortified by years of setbacks and letdowns. Yet, the flicker of hope I see in his expression threatens to climb over them.

"Let me try," he says simply. And those three words strike a chord in me, echoing around the empty chambers of a heart I thought was immune to such entreaties. "What do you want to know about me? I'll tell you anything you want to know."

The cool evening air brushes my cheeks, carrying with it the scent of motor oil and the heady tension between us. Wes's face is inches from mine, close enough that I can count the faint freckles scattered across his nose, a detail I'd never noticed before. His eyes, those deep wells of mischief, now hold something else—a vulnerability that's as disarming as it is unexpected.

"Let me prove it, Lara," he murmurs, and his breath is warm against my skin.

I should step back, break this spell before it tightens its grip any further. But I'm frozen, captivated by the earnest plea etched into the lines of his face, so different from the carefree smirk I'm used to. His hand reaches up, brushing a stray lock of hair behind my ear, and the gesture is so tender it nearly cracks the armor I've spent years building.

And then he leans in, slow and deliberate, giving me all the time in the world to retreat. But for a heartbeat, I don't want to. I want to know if his lips are as soft as they look, if that spark I feel is real or just a figment of my weary imagination. The space between us dwindles to nothing, and I can almost taste the kiss that's about to…

No. I place a hand on his chest, halting him mid-motion. "Wes, I… I need time to think," I say, my voice a hoarse whisper.

He pulls back, the corner of his mouth twitching in a half-smile that doesn't quite reach his eyes. "I get it," he says, but there's a note of disappointment there that tugs at something deep within me. "I don't like it, but I get it."

"Can I ask you something?" The question slips out before I can stop it—idle curiosity mingled with a desire to keep him near just a moment longer. "Veronica… how long were you two together?"

"Childhood sweethearts," he answers with a shrug, as if the weight of those words is lighter than air. "Pretty much grew up together. She's the reason I've been down lately. Trying to get back into my life again. But she was the one who cheated on me. Do I really want to open myself up to that again?"

Childhood sweethearts. The phrase echoes in my mind, painting a picture of Wes that doesn't fit with the playboy image he projects. It suggests depth, loyalty, the ability to commit. And *she* cheated on him? It might just be a story fabricated to win me over. But I see no lie in his face. He's never lied to me before. And if he could be with Veronica for that long, maybe—just maybe—he's capable of sincerity. Of wanting something real with me.

It's a dangerous thought, one that sets my heart racing for reasons I can't fully understand. I push it aside, focusing instead on the fact that he's here, right now, helping me when he doesn't have to.

"I understand. Thank you, Wes. For everything tonight," I say, retreating to the safety of my car, putting physical distance between the temptation he presents and the resolve I'm desperately clinging to.

"Does this have anything to do with Jamie?" Wes asks as I open the driver's door, and there's an edge to his voice that wasn't there before.

I slide into the driver's seat, avoiding his gaze, and close the door. "I don't think that's any of your business," I say, fumbling with the keys in the ignition.

"Sure," he says, leaning into the open window, and I can hear the skepticism. "I sense there's a lover's quarrel between you two."

I glare at him. "Not a lover's quarrel. We were friends. But…" *But you happened to screw it all up, Wes.* "We're not really talking right now."

"So I hear." There's a beat of silence where I expect him to say that he knows he's the reason. The players talk, and if Jamie sensed I had feelings for Wes, maybe everyone else has, too. But he doesn't. "Well, once you get your head screwed on straight, you know where to find me."

I power up the window, a welcome barrier to the conversation I'm not ready to have. As I pull away, the urge to slam my head against the steering wheel is overwhelming. I'm a mess of contradictions, caught between the past and the unpredictable possibility of a future with a man who might just be as complex as I am.

I drive off, leaving Wes—and my muddled thoughts—behind in the parking lot, the hum of the road ahead the only certainty I have left.

CHAPTER SIXTEEN

The air crackles with tension and the ice becomes a battleground as the Timberlake Titans clash with their rivals. I stand on the sidelines, my breath misting in the frosty air, eyes tracking every rapid movement. The echo of skates slashing across the slick surface fills the arena, punctuated by the sharp clack of sticks vying for control of the puck. The crowd is an entity of its own, a roaring force that ebbs and flows with the tide of the game.

My gaze follows Jamie as he maneuvers with an almost artistic precision, dodging opponents with a discipline that resonates from his days balancing academia and sports. His hair, a golden sweep beneath his helmet, is a stark contrast to the icy rink. Then there's "Wild" Wes, living up to his name with a boldness that borders on recklessness. He darts through the players, chaotic energy personified, his presence on the ice as disruptive as a storm.

The scoreboard looms overhead, a constant reminder of the high stakes as the clock ticks down, each second thumping in my chest like a drumbeat. The intensity of the game mirrors the pressure in my own career; these athletes rely on me, just as I once relied on the support of others when my sprinting dreams crumbled around me.

A sudden gasp from the crowd jerks my attention back to the game. In one heart-stopping moment, Jamie and Wes collide—two opposing forces meeting in a crash that seems to shake the very foundation of the arena. They both go down hard, sprawling on the ice amid a spray of frosty crystals. Time slows as the implications of their fall ripple through me.

I'm moving before I even register the decision, adrenaline pumping through my veins as I sprint toward the ice. My sneakers squeak against the polished floors, echoing the urgency that propels me forward.

When I get there, the two players are already being carried off the ice. Inside the PT area, I see Jamie and Wes being laid out on benches in separate rooms across from one another, pain etched into their features.

My hands are steady, but my mind races. As a former athlete turned sports therapist, understanding injury is second nature to me, but choosing whom to treat first? That's uncharted territory. Jamie lies still, his usual calm demeanor replaced by tight lines of discomfort around his mouth. Wes, unpredictable as ever, tries to sit up, wincing visibly.

"Stay put, Wes," I command, though my voice doesn't carry its usual authority.

Weighing the severity of their injuries feels like holding their careers—and my reputation—in my hands. If I get this wrong, I could exacerbate an injury, maybe even end one of their seasons prematurely. With Jamie's disciplined training, he might have avoided the worst, his body conditioned to take hits and recover quickly. Wes, however, is a wildcard; his unpredictable nature on the ice might translate to unpredictable injuries.

"Focus, Lara," I mutter to myself. There's no room for error here, no space for hesitation. I assess the angles of their bodies, the swelling, the potential strain on muscles and ligaments. Every second counts, and yet I can't rush this. I must choose wisely because it's not just their bodies that need mending—it's their trust in me to put them back together.

My gaze flickers between Jamie and Wes, the weight of my decision pressing down on me like the gravity of their fall. Wes's grimace is louder than Jamie's stoic silence, but it's the sharp angle of his leg that seals my choice. I step beside Wes first, not because he's louder or more animated, but because there's an urgency in the way he clutches at his knee, a silent alarm that speaks volumes to my trained eye.

"Looks like you're up, Wes," I say, trying to keep my tone light despite the pounding of my heart. "Let's see what you've done this time."

He attempts to flash me his trademark smirk, but pain wins out, crumpling his features. His flirtatious armor is dented, revealing a vulnerability he rarely shows on the ice. I focus on his injury, pushing aside the flutters in my stomach that come from being so close to his raw intensity. I can't afford to be swayed by his charms; there's a job to be done.

"Always getting into trouble, huh?" I quip as I palpate around his knee. He winces, but counters with a grin.

"Only when it means you'll touch me," he retorts, a spark of mischief in his eyes.

I roll my eyes, though a part of me warms to his teasing. It's classic Wes, using humor as a shield against discomfort. But beneath his words, there's an undercurrent of something more sincere, a need for reassurance that I'm here, that I've got him. I push harder on professionalism, ignoring the heat that threatens to distract me.

"Keep still," I instruct tersely, my fingers probing for signs of serious damage. Relief floods through me; it's not as bad as I feared. A possible sprain, not a tear. He'll be back on his feet sooner than expected, but right now, every second I spend with him feels like theft from Jamie's recovery time.

"Good news, Wes. It's just a sprain." I secure his knee with a practiced efficiency, wrapping it tightly but carefully. "You'll live to flirt another day."

"Can't wait," he answers, the cocky edge returning to his voice. But his eyes follow my movements with a confusion that doesn't match his confident facade. He's used to having my full attention, my care drawn out and personal. Today, it's strictly business.

"Almost done," I announce sooner than he expects, taking out my tape. "Let me just get it taped. Stay off it until I check it again, are we clear?"

"Crystal." There's a sharpness to his reply, a reaction to my abruptness.

"Good."

Outside, the buzzer goes off, signaling the end of the period. As I tape Wes's knee, I steel myself for Jamie's silent judgment. There's guilt in leaving Wes so quickly, but concern for Jamie propels me to move fast. Wes might have the louder personality, but right now, it's Jamie's quiet resilience that calls out to me the loudest.

Just as I'm taping the last fold over Wes's knee, the door slams open with a force that could rival the body checks happening on the ice. Pat stands on the threshold, her gaze like a slapshot straight to my conscience.

"Dammit, Lara! Why the hell isn't Jamie being seen to? He took a hard hit out there!"

I flinch, not from Pat's biting tone, but from the accusation that I've somehow failed in my duty. The Titans' bench is a revolving door of injuries and egos, but today, it feels like the weight of the entire game is pressing down on my shoulders.

"Jamie's next," I reply, pushing back against the urge to explain myself. "Wes's injury seemed more urgent. But I don't think he'll be back on the ice, at least for—"

"Seemed?" Pat arches an eyebrow, clearly unimpressed. "What made you think that? Make it quick. We need all hands on deck."

"Understood." I nod, trying to convey a confidence I don't feel.

Pat exits as abruptly as she entered, leaving a vacuum of silence that Wes fills with his own brand of brooding commentary.

"Rushing off to golden boy, huh?" Wes grumbles, shifting uncomfortably on the treatment table. His knee is secure now, but his pride seems bruised beyond repair.

"You heard Coach. Jamie needs to be looked at, Wes. You know how this works," I say, avoiding his gaze. My hands move of their own accord, cleaning up the scattered medical supplies with mechanical precision.

"Sure, sure," he retorts, bitterness lacing his voice. "Always the team player. But let's not forget who you saw first."

His words sting, but they also fuel a fire within me. A reminder that in this rink, I can't afford to play favorites—even if my heart disagrees.

"Maybe I'm saving the best for last. Rest up," I tell him, keeping it short and professional. "You'll be checked on again soon."

With one last glance at Wes, whose jaw is set in a hard line, I make my way to where Jamie is waiting.

The locker room is a maze of scattered gear and echoing curses, but I find Jamie sitting quietly, removed from the chaos. His leg is stretched out in front of him, and when our eyes meet, there's no blame in his gaze, only patience.

"Hey," I begin, kneeling beside him. "Sorry for the wait. I had to…"

I trail off. I don't want to mention Wes's name, since it's a definite sore spot.

"Hey, no worries." Jamie's voice is calm, soothing over the jagged edges of my guilt. "You're busy. And I'm fine."

"Are you?" I ask, grateful for Jamie's understanding nature. "Lie back. Let's see about you."

As I assess his condition, I'm struck by the quiet strength Jamie possesses. In the face of pain, there's no outcry for attention, no resentment—just a steady acceptance and trust that I'll do what's best. It's a stark contrast to Wes's fiery demeanor, and it makes me wonder about the balance between passion and peace, and where my heart truly lies on that spectrum.

I loosen the ties on his skates and pull them off, then roll down Jamie's hockey sock with careful, deliberate movements. Unstrapping the shin guard, I reveal a nasty bruise blooming across his shin, where the guard must've come loose. The skin is hot to the touch, and I wince in sympathy as my fingers lightly probe the area, assessing the damage.

It might be broken. He's definitely worse than Wes.

"Doesn't look too good," I murmur, reaching for the medical kit beside me.

"It's not so bad," Jamie says, but his jaw clenches tight, betraying his stoicism. I don't know if he's putting on the stiff upper lip because he doesn't want to show pain, or because he's still sore at me and doesn't want to show any emotion to me.

As I'm rifling around the bag, he slumps against me, his eyes unfocused, giving me a jolt of fear. I grab a nearby plastic container just in time for him to vomit.

Concussion. His condition is rapidly deteriorating. "Whoa, hold on here," I say, holding his head still so I can look in his eyes. They're unfocused. "I think we need to get you to the hospital for some X-rays."

He blinks hard and reaches for his head as I settle him down. "Shit. I don't feel so well."

"Yeah, that's what happens when you nearly lose your head," I tell him lightly. But guilt twists in my gut as I call for the paramedics—I should have been here sooner. Jamie needs someone who doesn't second-guess his pain, who doesn't prioritize the loud over the quiet. Yet, here he sits, offering nothing but understanding while I replay the could-have-beens in my head. I can't help but think that, in another life, without my past clouding my judgment, I would've seen Jamie first.

"I'm going to wrap this up and put some ice on it," I tell him, my hands steady even as my conscience falters. "To reduce the swelling. Then you're heading to the hospital for those X-rays and observation. Okay?"

"Thanks, Lara." He watches me work, his eyes reflecting a calm sea in which I find myself momentarily adrift.

"Jamie, I—" The words catch in my throat, but I force them out. "I'm sorry. For earlier. I…"

"Hey." His hand is warm on mine, halting my movements. "You don't need to apologize to me. For anything. It's forgiven."

His reassurance should ease the weight on my shoulders, but instead, it adds a different kind of heaviness—one that comes from recognizing the depth of his kindness. And now, there is something between Wes and me, however slight and fleeting. Regret taps at my heart. How did I get so lucky to be caught between two men so wildly different, yet both incredible in their own right?

"Still," I say, focusing again on wrapping his leg, "I didn't mean to make you wait. I shouldn't have taken your patience for granted."

"Hey, it's fine." He chuckles softly, a sound that somehow manages to be both comforting and heart-wrenching.

The tape secures the bandage in place, and I reach for an ice pack, nestling it against the bruise. His flinch is slight, but I notice it, and my resolve strengthens. No more taking Jamie for granted—no more overlooking the silent strength he embodies.

"Try not to move too much," I instruct, meeting his gaze. "Give it time to heal."

"Like your sprinter's leg?" His question carries a weight, a tether to my own history of hurt and recovery.

"Exactly like that," I admit, a sad smile playing on my lips. "Had to learn the hard way that time and care are the best medicine."

"Then I'm in good hands." His eyes hold mine, and something unspoken passes between us—a promise, perhaps, or an acknowledgment of the bond we're building, one careful treatment at a time.

As I pack up my supplies, the tightness in my chest loosens a fraction. Maybe it's okay to feel guilty for a moment if it leads to growth—if it reminds you not to overlook the quiet strength that often goes unseen. And maybe, just maybe, it's a sign that my heart is still open, still capable of learning how to choose not just the urgent, but also the important.

CHAPTER SEVENTEEN

My heart flutters in my chest as I stand outside Pat Lawson's office, the dull throb of anxiety pulsing through me. My fingers nervously twist a rogue strand of hair that's escaped my practical ponytail. The silence in the corridor feels oppressive, thick with the weight of impending confrontation.

The door swings open, and there she is—Pat Lawson, her face etched with lines of disapproval that seem to deepen with every stern glance she throws my way. "Lara Bennett," she calls out, her voice sharp and commanding, cutting through the tension like a slap. I step forward, trying to ground myself in the confidence that used to carry me across finish lines.

"Have a seat," she says without a hint of warmth. I comply, perching on the edge of the hard-backed chair as if ready for a quick getaway. Her eyes, hawk-like, fixate on me, and suddenly, I'm not just Lara Bennett, sports therapist; I'm Lara Bennett, the accused.

"I'm sure you know why I called you in here," Pat starts, folding her arms as if bracing herself for battle. "You're undermining team dynamics with your favoritism."

I meet her gaze, my eyes steady, even if my heart is not. "I don't play favorites, Coach," I say firmly. "Each player has individual needs. As a former athlete, I understand the nuances of their physical challenges. My decisions are always about what's best for their recovery and performance."

"Yes, but it turns out that Jamie's injury and concussion was far more serious than Wes's. And after the rumors I've heard about you two, I have to wonder whether you're thinking about what is best for each individual player," she counters skeptically, questioning the very foundation of my expertise. "And for the team as a whole."

"I know there have been rumors," I concede, "but they are just that. Rumors. Second-hand gossip about—"

"Carter is the one talking it up. I call that first-hand information."

My stomach drops. Of course he was. Taking a deep breath, I collect my thoughts.

"If he has been, he's exaggerating. It really amounts to nothing."

"Dr. Bennett, I don't need a temptress leading my players on. Their one focus needs to be on the ice. Not on their therapist."

It hits me like a slap. A temptress? I've never even worn a low-cut blouse before. I open my mouth to tell her that, but then I stop. I told them both I wanted to stay professional, but have my actions shown that? Have I led them on?

If I had, then I'm not an asset to the team. I'm a detriment. And that means that she has every right to…

Oh no. I suck in a breath.

"My personal life does not interfere with my training as a sports therapist. I assess, I plan, and I adapt based on what each player requires." I lean forward slightly, driven by the need to make her understand. "It's never personal. It's professional. And I may have made the wrong judgment call, but it wasn't because of favoritism. It was…naivete."

Pat's expression remains unreadable, but I sense the gears turning behind those calculating eyes. She's old-school hockey through and through, and I'm the new variable she can't quite figure out. Yet here I am, standing my ground, because this isn't just about defending my methods—it's about standing up for this career that I have come to love more than anything.

"The truth is," Lawson said, "I just spoke to Jamie's doctor, and though his shin isn't broken, his concussion is one of several he's had. He has to be careful, because one more might be the end of his career. Because of that…"

I stare, speechless. "But…there wasn't any real way of knowing. Anyone could've made the same mistake."

"I spoke to Jamie, too. He seems to think that favoritism was involved."

I can't believe what I'm hearing. *Jamie* said that? After telling me he didn't hold it against me? "I don't understand. He told me it was okay. He wasn't showing signs of a concussion when they took him off the ice. It was only when—"

"I understand," she says, her voice firm. "I was going to suggest we end your contract early and get another doctor in here. But that'll take some time. I'm willing to reconsider my stance. Lara, you've got another shot, but I'm keeping a close eye on things. Don't mess up again."

I let out a breath I didn't realize I was holding, a weight lifting off my shoulders while doubt continues to swirl. Why would Jamie throw me under the bus like that? I thought he didn't hold the past against me. As I stand up from the rigid chair, my legs are shaky, but not from weakness—rather from a sudden surge of relief and determination. I can still make a difference here; I can still prove that my methods work.

"Thank you, Pat. I won't let you down," I promise, my voice steadier than I feel.

Once outside the office, the corridor seems too narrow for the storm of emotions swirling inside me. I need to move, to walk it off, but before I can take a step, Jamie is there, leaning against his crutches with a world of hurt etched on his face. It's a surprise, seeing him so soon after the injury. The second he sees me, he starts to limp away. I skip into a run to catch up to him.

"Jamie, I—" I begin. "What was that all about?"

He stops and gazes at me so coldly, the hallway suddenly feels even smaller, his presence filling up the space. I nod, urging him to continue.

"I know you have feelings for Wes," he says quietly, and my stomach tightens at the mention of Wes's name. "And I get it, he's… well, he's Wes. But I've been the nice guy, staying on the sidelines, hoping you'll see me the same way. But you're never going to, right?"

His words hit me like a punch, leaving me breathless and without an answer. Jamie's gaze searches mine, looking for a truth I'm not ready to confront.

The pause is one beat too long.

"Never mind," he says, a hint of resignation creeping into his voice as he straightens up. "I think I got my answer."

"Jamie, I—" I start, but the words knot up in my throat.

He gives me a sad sort of smile, one that doesn't quite reach his eyes, and I know I've hurt him without saying a word.

I reach out, my fingers twitching with the urge to comfort him, to smooth over the hurt I've caused, but I stop myself. Touching him now would be another false promise, another breadcrumb leading nowhere.

"Save it, Lara." He cuts me off, the gentle tone he always used with me now laced with a quiet firmness. "It's okay. Really, I should've seen it. But I was an idiot."

He turns away, the crutches squeaking faintly as he begins to move down the hallway. Each step he takes echoes in the empty space, punctuating the end of something that never truly began.

"Jamie!" I call out, my heart racing, but he doesn't turn around. I watch as he shakes his head, a silent concession to the reality we both knew, but only one of us was willing to admit.

CHAPTER EIGHTEEN

I watch the players glide across the ice, their breaths visible in the chilly air as they collide and compete. The practice is intense, but there's an edge to it today that sets my nerves on edge. Now that his minor injury has healed, Wes is a force to be reckoned with, barreling through drills with a ferocity that doesn't go unnoticed. I wince every time he body-checks someone, knowing I'm going to have to deal with it later in the therapy room.

"Easy there, Carter!" Coach yells out, but Wes doesn't let up. He's like a storm, relentless and unyielding, and it sends a shiver down my spine—a mixture of awe and concern.

A twinge of guilt tightens in my chest as I glance over to the bench. I see the way Jamie's jaw clenches, the focus in his eyes overshadowed by something darker. It's my fault. If only I'd been able to give him the reassurance he sought from me, maybe he wouldn't be in such a world of hurt. But I couldn't lie to him—not when my heart is so torn.

The whistle blows, signaling the start of another play, and I seize the moment to approach Jamie on the bench.

"Jamie," I begin, my voice steady despite the tremor I feel within. "How are you feeling today?"

His leg stretched out in front of him, he turns to face me, and I'm met with the intensity of his gaze. There's a beat, a silence that stretches too thin before he replies, "I'm benched, aren't I?"

"Yes, but if you keep with therapy, you could be back for playoffs."

Jamie scoffs, a hollow sound that echoes off the ice. "Six weeks from now. Great."

He turns away, ignoring me.

"Jamie. Come on. I know you hate me after what I did, but I'm sorry. Can't you forgive me?" I ask, a little more sharply than I intended. My hands clench at my sides, aching for something to hold onto.

"There's nothing to forgive. You like Wes better." Jamie's voice rises, betraying the calm facade he's been holding as he stares out onto the ice, watching the play. "I'm not a child, Lara. I don't hold grudges."

Maybe he won't admit it, but I sense that's a lie. "Jamie, I—"

"No, Lara. I get it." His words are hot, each one stinging as they hit. "You made your choice clear when you went to him before checking on anyone else. And now, I'm paying the price."

"Jamie, that's not fair," I argue back, feeling my own anger flare up. I hate that he thinks I chose Wes over him. That's not how it was. "I'm a sports therapist. I went to who I thought needed me most. I thought you understood that."

"Sure," he snaps, sarcasm tinging his tone. "And I'm forgotten. As usual. The nice guy comes in last."

"Stop it, Jamie," I plead, my voice cracking. This isn't us. I can't help longing for those days of connection and easy conversation. They seem long gone. "Please. Can't we call a truce?"

He snorts. "Sure. So I can watch you and Wes riding off into the sunset?"

I stare in disbelief. "That's stupid. I don't—"

"Oh, bullshit. You're in love with him. You look at him in a way you've never looked at me. And I'm not going to pretend to be fine with it."

I stare at the ground, unable to find the words.

"Look, I thought I could handle it, okay?" Jamie throws his hands up in exasperation. "I thought I could be the nice guy. But seeing you with him, knowing what he is to you—it kills me."

"Jamie—" My throat feels tight, words still failing me.

He shakes his head, the hurt clear in his eyes. "Right," he says, his laugh hollow. "It's always Wes who needs you. Treats you like shit, injects all the drama. And you like that. Admit it."

"Jamie, it's not like that," I insist, feeling the weight of every pair of eyes on us. The cold of the rink seeps into my bones, but it's nothing compared to the chill in Jamie's gaze.

"Isn't it?" His eyes search mine, looking for something I'm not sure I can give. "You always find a way to be there for him, Lara. When does it become more about choice than obligation?"

"Jamie, no, that's not what I meant—"

But he rises to his feet, using his crutches to propel himself up the steps and out of the arena. He doesn't look back. The players, silent sentinels to our unraveling, return to their drills with a tension that matches the one knotting in my stomach.

The practice ends, and I go to find him, hoping for a second chance to explain, to make things right. But Jamie is nowhere to be found. Alone, I gather my kit, my heart heavy.

Outside, the sky is dark and foreboding, mirroring my tumultuous thoughts. No sooner do I step out than rain pelts down, soaking me within moments.

I rush to the car and get inside, then start the engine. It sputters. Idiot that I am, I never got it fixed, even after almost getting stranded last month. Now is a hell of a time to have to brave the elements, but I have no choice. I'm the last car in the parking lot. Stranded.

With a sigh, I set off on foot, each step squelching in my soggy shoes.

Headlights cut through the downpour, and a car eases up beside me. I walk faster, ignoring it even as it follows me. It's only when the window powers down that I realize it's Wes.

"Get in, Lara. You're drenched," he urges, but I shake my head, pressing forward.

"Thanks, but I'll walk," I tell him, unable to bear the thought of another entanglement with either of them today.

"Come on, don't be ridiculous." There's an edge to his voice, frustration or maybe something more. "I heard about what happened with Jamie. Let's talk about it."

"Please, Wes, just go." I don't stop walking, even as the rain blurs my vision.

He falls silent, and for a moment, I think he's driven away. But when I glance back, he's still there, his expression unreadable as the storm rages around us.

The relentless rain shows no mercy as my pace quickens, the waterlogged path ahead of me a blur. Suddenly, the car door slams shut behind me—the sharp sound a stark counterpoint to the storm's dull roar. I don't have to look to know Wes has gotten out; the air shifts with his presence, electric and charged, as he falls into step beside me.

"Dammit, Lara, stop being so stubborn," he growls, his voice barely rising above the pitter-patter of raindrops pelting the pavement.

I whirl around, my eyes flashing fire in the twilight gloom, meeting his gaze. The rain has plastered his dark hair to his forehead, and his clothes cling to his muscular frame, just as drenched as I am. For a moment, we're suspended in time, the world reduced to the space between us, crackling with silent acknowledgment of the chaos our lives have become.

“Leave me alone, Wes,” I spit out, the words tasting bitter on my tongue. “You’re why everything’s such a mess.”

His eyes darken, the roguish grin that usually plays on his lips now nowhere in sight. “Me? You think this is all on me?” His hands ball into fists at his sides, and even through the downpour, I can see the tension coiling in his posture like a spring.

“Isn’t it?” My voice breaks, betraying the turmoil within. “Ever since you showed up, my life’s been turned upside down!”

“Because I made you feel something?” He steps closer, the heat of his body cutting through the chill of the rain. “Because, for once, you weren’t in control?”

“Exactly!” I shout, my heart hammering against my ribs. “Because I can’t—I don’t want to—”

Our heated gazes lock, and the air between us thrums with unsaid words and unspent desire. It’s a magnetic force, drawing us inexorably together until the distance evaporates. Then, without warning, his lips crash against mine, fierce and demanding. My mind screams to push him away, but my body betrays me, melting into his embrace as if pulled by the tide.

Wes’s hands find their way to my waist, pulling me closer, and I’m lost in the sensation of rain and touch, heat and cold, anger and longing. Our breaths mingle, hot against the coolness of the rain, as the kiss deepens and the rest of the world fades away. For those fleeting moments, there’s nothing else—no Jamie, no guilt, just Wes and the overwhelming tumult of emotions he stirs within me.

My fingers thread through his damp hair, holding him to me with a desperation I didn’t know I possessed. The rain continues to pour, oblivious to the unraveling of my self-control, each drop mingling with the warmth of our skin, forging rivulets that cascade over us like shared secrets.

But even as our bodies press closer in the tempest, reality claws at the edges of my consciousness, reminding me of the consequences, the hurt, the impossible decisions that lie in wait. It’s a battle I’m not sure I’m prepared to fight, not here, not now, caught in the eye of the storm with Wes Carter.

Breathless, I shove away from him, gasping for air as if I’ve been submerged underwater. Rain pelts us, indifferent to the chaos it’s witnessed, continuing its relentless descent. We’re both drenched to the bone, shivering from the raw intensity that crackles between us like a live wire.

He reaches out, as though to pull me back, but I step out of his grasp, my heart thundering against my ribs with a ferocity that rivals the storm around us. Our eyes meet—his hazel gaze is clouded with something akin to desperation, mirroring the tumultuous whirlwind churning inside me.

"I hate you," I choke out, the words slicing through the downpour like shards of ice. My voice trembles, betraying the turmoil that rips through my chest. I can feel every drop trace the contours of my face, mingling with the hot tears that threaten to spill over. "But I can't stop this."

It's a confession torn from the deepest part of me—a place I've kept guarded, a secret even from myself until this very moment. His expression shifts, hurt and understanding warring in his eyes. He knows the weight of these words, knows what it costs me to admit them.

Wes steps closer, and I can almost taste the intensity of his presence. But I can't let him bridge the gap again—not when every inch of space between us is charged with the electricity of our connection.

"I don't know what to do," I whisper, more to myself than to him. The admission hangs between us, heavy and suffocating. The rain continues its unyielding symphony, pounding on the pavement, soaking through my clothes, chilling me to the core.

For a long moment, neither of us moves, the space between us a battlefield where heartache and longing collide. Then, with a ragged breath, he backs away, his jaw clenched tight, as if holding back words that might shatter the fragile silence.

I watch him retreat, each step he takes splashing water that reflects the streetlights' hazy glow. And there, under the veil of the evening downpour, I stand alone, grappling with the war within—a love that feels like hate, a need that feels like despair, and a heart that doesn't know which way to turn.

CHAPTER NINETEEN

The harsh glow of my phone screen is the only light in the dimness of my workspace. I'm sitting at the desk in the corner, alone, the silence a thick blanket around me, when the notification pops up—an alert from one of those gossip sites that feed on scandal. My finger hovers, hesitates, then taps. There it is—me and Jamie, mid-argument rinkside, our faces twisted with anger, our words a cacophony that now screams across the internet. Someone at the rink must've found our argument worth taking video of, and now it's gone viral.

"Can't believe that bitch would talk like that to our boy Jamie! She's the stupid one. #Disappointed" flashes across my feed, followed by a string of others, each one a punch to the gut.

Did I call him stupid? Apparently. I can't remember. The whole thing is a blur; the only thing that sticks in my mind is the look of hurt and betrayal etched on Jamie's face.

I'm definitely the bad guy in this fight. Fans, people who don't even know me, are shredding my character based on a few heated seconds. A lump forms in my throat as my eyes catch on a particularly venomous comment: "What an utter disgrace to the team."

My hands tremble, the phone nearly slipping through my fingers. It's ridiculous how these pixels, these bits of virtual vitriol, can feel like actual blows.

I draw in a deep breath, trying to steady myself. The old sprinter's discipline kicks in. *Focus on what you can control, Lara.* But right now, everything feels like it's spinning out of control.

The ice offers no respite. As I step down toward the rink, the air seems to thicken, charged with unspoken recriminations. Team members glance my way, their eyes darting off just as quickly. I'm used to being greeted with smiles, claps on the back, but today I might as well be wading through a mire of awkward silences.

"Did you see the video?"

"Who the hell does she think she is?"

Their whispers reach me, unintended yet cutting. The voices belong to figures in the distance, their backs turned to me as if I were contagious. They're questioning my loyalty, the very thing I've dedicated my life to bolstering. For a moment, I'm frozen, a spectator to their doubt. And then, the therapist in me takes over—I push forward, determined to do the job I came here to do, despite the whispers, despite the looks.

Even so, I feel the tears coming. This is my job. I'm supposed to be a professional. And now, for some reason, the whole world hates me because I've hurt America's Golden Boy. Of course, they'd be on his side. He's amazing. And I'm the stupid one.

I pivot on my heel and slip into the supply room, a sanctuary from the whispers and wary glances. Safe in the solitude, I release a breath I didn't realize I was holding—until strong arms envelop me from behind, turning me around, and a pair of lips crash against mine.

"Jesus, Wes!" I gasp, jerking away with a mix of anger and shock. My back hits the wall of jerseys and deflated soccer balls, creating a dull thud that echoes my racing heart. "What are you doing?"

"Showing support," he says with a roguish grin that infuriates me more. His hand still hovers in the air where my waist just was, as if he's reluctant to let go of the connection.

"Support doesn't come with an ambush kiss," I snap, brushing past him, feeling the wicked witch in their story. "And it's not what I need right now."

"Hey, don't let them get to you," Wes says, his voice earnest for once. He leans against a shelf, a casual pose that belies the intensity in his eyes. "I've been the bad guy before, remember? It can be fun if you don't take it all so seriously."

"Fun?" My hands ball into fists at my sides. "Is that what this is to you? Just fun?"

He shrugs. "No…that's not what I meant. What I meant is, to hell with what other people think. If we're happy…"

"Happy?" I snort. That's not what I am right now. Far from it. "And there's nothing fun about this, Wes. I hurt someone I care about. Unlike you, I can't just shrug off being vilified. You're the Titans' star player. They need you. Me? There are a thousand other PTs that could take my place tomorrow. I have to remain professional."

"Professional, right," he murmurs, something flickering across his expression—hurt, maybe, but it's gone as quickly as it came. He straightens up, the smirk returning to his face like armor. "Because Miss Perfect Professional hasn't made any mistakes. Maybe Jamie doesn't deserve your sympathy. Maybe he needs to grow a pair and realize he can't win them all."

His words cut deep, a verbal slap that echoes the physical sting of the kiss. I flinch, knowing he meant to hit where it hurts, and he knows he's scored a direct hit.

I hold up a hand as I head for the door.

"Where are you going?" he demands, but I give him a warning look.

I march down the corridor, my resolve steeling with each step. The door to the locker room is ajar, and I see him there—Jamie's sitting in the locker room on the bench, his light hair glinting under the fluorescent lights. My heart throbs painfully against my ribcage; this might be my last chance to clear the air.

"Jamie." My voice barely carries above a whisper, but it's enough. He looks up, and for a moment, his eyes lock onto mine before turning cold, an arctic barrier slamming down between us. I edge into the room, acutely aware of the space he puts between us, as if my presence is something to endure rather than welcome. "I just wanted to tell you..."

He leans back a little, arms crossed, the epitome of detachment. "What's there to talk about, Lara? The whole world has seen your side of the story."

"Please." I reach out, but it's like trying to touch a reflection—he's close but untouchable. I take a deep breath, fighting the tide of emotions threatening to break free. "I'm sorry, Jamie. For the argument, for everything that's been blown out of proportion. I never meant to make this about me."

His gaze doesn't waver, but it doesn't warm either. "Your intentions don't change the outcome, Lara. The team...they're rattled. They don't trust you, and neither do I."

"Is there no way I can fix this?" The question hangs between us, heavy and ominous.

"Right now, I think it's best if you just focus on your work and make it through the season." His voice is crisp, professional, and utterly devoid of the warmth I once knew.

The finality in his tone reverberates through me. I've fully ruined things. At the end of the season, I will be out of a job. I nod, unable to muster another word, and back out of the room. The door closes with a soft click, a quiet punctuation to the conversation—no, the confrontation—that leaves me hollowed out.

Back in the solitude of the therapy room, I sink onto a bench. My hands are steady now, but inside, a storm brews. No allies, no confidants, just an echoing silence where camaraderie used to live. I press the heels of my palms into my eyes, willing away the sting of tears.

"Just get through this," I murmur to myself, a mantra to anchor my drifting thoughts. These people, their opinions—they're not the measure of my worth. I've overcome injury, disappointment, and loss. This is just another hurdle.

Slowly, I stand, rolling my shoulders back and lifting my chin. I am Lara Bennett, former sprinter turned top-notch sports therapist. I won't let their whispers dictate my pace. I'll run this race alone if I have to, and I'll cross the finish line with my head held high.

CHAPTER TWENTY

My heart races like it's back on the track, each beat a reminder of what's at stake tonight. I sit alone at a corner table in the upscale restaurant, fidgeting with the hem of my dress—a sartorial departure from my usual sportswear. The fabric is a nod to the calm I'm desperately trying to channel. Wes's text glows on my phone screen, its apologetic words looping in my mind.

Sorry about earlier. Dinner on me to make up for it? it reads.

I replay the message for the hundredth time, hoping it will quell the nervous energy coursing through me. It's not often that "Wild" Wes, known for his carefree swagger and his ability to dodge commitment like a skilled fullback, offers such a concession. I scan the room, searching for the familiar figure that's haunted both my professional reserve and my unbidden dreams.

The clink of cutlery and the low hum of conversation act as a soundtrack to my anticipation. I've been here before—waiting, always waiting—for something or someone to alter the course of my carefully constructed life. But this is different. This is personal.

Suddenly, the room shifts. Heads turn, and murmurs rise like a wave as Wes strides into the restaurant. He's impossible to miss—the casual confidence, the athletic build barely contained by his dark shirt, the rakish smile that's disarmed many before me. His eyes lock onto mine, and he approaches with an easy gait that is the very opposite of the tension I feel.

"Hey, Lara," he says, his voice warm and inviting, as if we're old friends rather than romantic partners caught in an emotional tangle.

"Hi, Wes," I manage, my voice steady despite the fluttering in my chest.

His smile widens, genuine and surprisingly vulnerable, reaching his eyes and carving dimples into his cheeks. It's a look that's rare for him, reserved and now bestowed upon me. For a moment, I forget the reason we're here, the apology hanging between us like a delicate truce.

"Thanks for this," I say as he takes his seat across from me.

"Of course. I feel like I should do something nice for you, after all the stuff I've put you through," Wes replies, his gaze holding mine with an intensity that sends a thrill down my spine. There's something electric in the air as we navigate this unfamiliar territory, our usual banter set aside for something more sincere. "Hope you like Italian."

"Love it," I confess, allowing myself a moment to marvel at how easily a smile can transform his face. It's as if the bad boy facade slips, revealing hints of the man beneath who might just care enough to try making amends.

My fingers trace the edge of my napkin, twirling it into a tight spiral as Wes clears his throat. The restaurant's warm glow seems to dim slightly, anticipation hanging heavily in the air. I look up, catching the hesitation that flickers across his features.

"Can I be honest with you?" he begins, and there's an earnestness in his voice that commands my full attention. "When I see something I want, I take it. And I want you, Lara. But you're the first thing I've ever wanted that hasn't bent to my wishes. And that excites me. You're all I ever think about. Do you know that?"

His confession sends a ripple of warmth through me, yet it stirs a cauldron of my own fears and reservations. We sit in the echo of his words, the clinking of silverware and muted conversations around us fading into the background.

Taking a deep breath, I finally speak. "Wes, I appreciate your honesty. But I need you to know where I stand too." I steel myself, locking onto his gaze. "I'm not looking for a relationship with anyone on the team right now. My career is everything to me. It's what I've poured all of my energy into after—"

The memory of my injury, the end of my sprinting dreams, flares up, but I push it aside. "After everything," I finish, firmly.

There's a pause as Wes digests my words, the intensity in his eyes never wavering. "That's what I like about you. You know what you want, too. So we don't have to put labels on it. Can't we just have a good time together and see where this goes?"

A mutual understanding settles over us, fragile yet profound. Neither of us ready to leap into the unknown, yet unable to ignore the pull that's undeniably drawing us together.

"I guess," I say, but it's only when those words are out that I wonder if they're really true. Is that really what I'm looking for? A fire that burns itself out after a season? Or do I want something more?

Silence lingers, a mute accord that we're both treading uncharted waters, navigating the currents of attraction and the hazards of our personal demons.

In that silence, though, I think of Jamie, and my heart does a little dance. He and I were building toward something, and the thought of that had made me so happy. But now…it's gone.

And all I have is Wes. Fun, no commitment, hot as hell Wes.

The rest of dinner is nice, full of flirtatious banter and delicious Italian food. It's pleasant, but I can't shake the feeling that something is missing. I tell myself I'm having a great time, but for some reason, it feels hollow. Like a lie. As much as I try not to think of him, Jamie's image keeps intruding, his expression full of hurt.

When the waiter slides the check across the polished mahogany tabletop, interrupting the taut silence that has settled between us. Wes reaches for it with a fluid motion, his fingers brushing mine, sending an unexpected jolt through my arm. I pull away, more from surprise than anything else, and watch him deftly place his credit card on the tray without glancing at the total.

"Thank you for dinner," I murmur, feeling the weight of this gesture. Does this mean he expects something in return tonight?

"Least I could do," he replies, the corners of his mouth lifting in a half-smile that doesn't quite reach his eyes. There's a tension there, a wariness that wasn't present when we first sat down.

The waiter returns, Wes signs the receipt with a quick flourish, and we stand together, the motion synchronized as if we've done this a hundred times before. The subtle brush of his hand against my back as we navigate through the tables feels intimate, deliberate. I'm hyperaware of his proximity, the heat radiating from him.

"Ready?" he asks, his voice low.

"Ready," I echo, nearly breathless.

We push through the heavy door of the restaurant and step out into the night. The evening air is cool, a stark contrast to the warmth we leave behind. It wraps around me like a whisper, making me shiver slightly. Above us, streetlights cast a soft golden glow on the sidewalk, painting everything with a gentle luminescence.

Wes pauses beside me, and I sense him turning, his gaze fixing on me with an intensity that sends another wave of shivers down my spine. I meet his eyes, letting myself get lost for a moment in their hazel depths. They reflect the streetlights, flecks of gold and green dancing within them.

“You want to go to my place?” he asks huskily, a note of concern threading through his words.

I nod, not trusting my voice. There is a storm of emotions brewing inside me. His presence is overwhelming, suffocating in its allure.

He steps closer, and I can’t help but take a small step back, my back hitting the cool brick wall of the building. There’s nowhere to go, and suddenly, I’m under the Wes spell. I don’t want to be anywhere else. His hand comes up, hovering in the space between us, and I wonder if he’s going to touch me, to bridge the gap that’s both physical and emotional.

“Look at me, Lara,” he says softly, and I realize I’ve been staring at his chest, unable to face the full force of what’s in his eyes. The magnetic pull is undeniable, drawing me toward him with the promise of something neither of us can quite name. My heart races, thundering in my ears, matching the rhythm of the city around us. We are alone here in this cocoon of light and shadow, the rest of the world momentarily forgotten.

The space between us evaporates. His lips crash against mine in a breathless wave. I respond, emboldened by desire and the night’s intoxicating atmosphere. Wes’s kiss deepens, stirring a warmth that cascades through my body, setting every nerve ending ablaze. My hands find their way to his hair, soft strands slipping between my fingers. The world falls away; it’s just Wes and me, and the promise of what might be, here in the sheltered alcove of the restaurant’s side entrance.

Yes, this is what I want, I tell myself, letting my every nerve make the decision instead of my heart. Because I think it is trying to tell me something else, and I’m afraid of what.

CHAPTER TWENTY ONE

I push the door open, the metallic scent of sweat and liniment hitting me like an unwelcome wave. The locker room is quiet, unnervingly so. It's as if my entrance has sucked the noise right out of the space. My heart pounds against my ribcage, thrumming a frantic rhythm that I can't seem to control. I tell myself it's adrenaline from work, from being in this place of competition and athletic prowess, but deep down, I know it's more than that. It's about him—Jamie.

The air is thick with something unspoken, the lingering tension between us palpable like a physical barrier. Each step feels heavier than the last, the echoes of my sneakers on the tiled floor resonating too loudly in the silence. My eyes scan the rows of lockers, some standing open, revealing glimpses of lives contained in small metal boxes. And then they find him.

Jamie's leaning back against his locker, arms crossed over his chest—a picture of casual indifference. But his gaze locks onto mine the moment I step fully into the room, and I swear I see the flicker of something more behind those eyes. Something he's quick to hide.

"Looks like our star therapist is making headlines off the ice." Jamie's voice cuts through the quiet, sharp as a knife. His words are light, but there's a bite to them that makes my skin prickle. "Heard you and Wes are together now."

He might have heard it, but it doesn't make it true. That night, after dinner, I told Wes I needed more time. I left him at the door to his apartment with a chaste kiss on the cheek, telling him I'd find my way home. Sure, he was confused, but no more confused than I am right now.

But Jamie's looking at me like I've committed some kind of terrible crime. And yes, I'm guilty of playing with his heart while trying to figure out my own. It still doesn't warrant *this*.

I square my shoulders, the resolve building inside me like a storm. I've had enough of the tension, the sarcasm, enough of Jamie poking at wounds that are far from healed. "Jamie," I start, my voice surprisingly steady despite the maelstrom of emotions whirling within me. "This thing you're doing—this passive-aggressive commentary—it has to stop."

Jamie's face, so often a mask of composure, falters as he sees something in my eyes that gives him pause. The smirk that had been his armor slowly dissipates, replaced by a vulnerability I haven't seen in him in a while. He steps closer, the air between us charged with a history of unsaid words and stifled feelings.

"Look, Lara…" His voice is thick with emotion, a stark contrast to the cool detachment that had laced his words moments before. "I know I've been… harsh. But it's only because seeing you with him—I don't get it. It hurts like hell. I thought you and I had something. Was I wrong?"

No, he wasn't wrong.

"Jamie, I—" My response is cut short as the locker room door slams open, the sound reverberating off the walls.

Wes strides in, his presence like a sudden storm cloud darkening the day. He doesn't say anything, but he doesn't need to—the shift in the atmosphere speaks volumes. My heart, already tumultuous, skips erratically. Conflicting waves of guilt and desire crash within me, each glance toward Wes a silent admission of the tangled emotions I can't seem to unravel.

Jamie's jaw clenches, his body tensing as if bracing against an invisible blow. I watch helplessly as the openness that had flickered across his face seconds ago hardens into a shield of restraint. His eyes, once alight with the spark of vulnerability, now scan the room with a steely edge, gauging Wes's reaction, measuring the distance between us all.

The tension coils tighter, a tangible entity that fills the room to the brim, leaving no space for escape. Wes's eyes meet mine, a silent conversation passing between us—one filled with questions and accusations, promises and regrets. His gaze shifts to Jamie, acknowledging the change, the line we'd all crossed without even moving.

Time stretches into an endless void, the silence in the locker room a thick blanket suffocating every breath. We stand there—Jamie, Wes, and I—each of us ensnared by the snarl of emotions that tethers us together yet keeps us painfully apart. The air feels electric with tension, charged with words unsaid and feelings uncharted. My pulse hammers in my ears, drowning out all other sounds, as if the very rhythm of my heart betrays my turmoil.

“Seems like I missed quite the show.” Wes’s voice slices through the silence, rough-edged and dripping with a bitterness that doesn’t quite mask the hurt beneath. His eyes, those turbulent pools of hazel, lock onto mine with an intensity that threatens to unravel me. Then they flicker to Jamie, the implied challenge unmistakable.

“Wasn’t a performance,” Jamie retorts, his tone rigidly controlled but simmering with an undercurrent of raw emotion. “Every word I’ve ever told her has been real.”

The words hang suspended, adding weight to the already stifling atmosphere. I swallow hard, my throat tight, feeling as though I’m caught in the eye of a storm, where the slightest movement could bring everything crashing down around us.

“Real?” Wes scoffs, one corner of his mouth twisting up into a wry smile that doesn’t reach his eyes.

“Yeah. Something you know nothing about. Always playing it up for the camera,” Jamie bites out, rising to his feet and shoving his crutches away to come toe-to-toe with Wes.

“Enough,” I whisper, more to myself than to them. The word is a plea for sanity, a call for calm in the midst of chaos. But it echoes off the lockers, sounding like a command even to my own ears.

I take a deep, steadying breath, and when I speak, my voice is firmer. “I can see the pain I’ve caused both of you, and I’m sorry.” My gaze shifts between the two men who have unexpectedly come to mean so much to me. “Jamie, your honesty… it means the world to me. And Wes, your boldness has always been something I admired, even when it scares me.”

They’re both watching me now, their expressions guarded, waiting for the words that will tip the scales. I feel it—the decision I must make, pressing against the walls of my chest, demanding release.

“Choices,” I say, the word tasting bitter on my tongue. “Every day we make them. Some are easy, like what to wear or what to eat. Others… others can change the course of our lives.”

My fingers clench at my sides, nails digging into my palms to anchor me to this moment. I sound so stupid. Who am I to lecture them after the mess I’ve made with their hearts?

“What I’m trying to say is…” I pause, searching for the courage that seems just out of reach. “I care about both of you. But I can’t do this anymore. I have a job to do. And I need to concentrate on that. So *please*…let’s just stop all this.”

Jamie's stance softens, a silent nod acknowledging my plea. Wes's jaw clenches, his pride warring with the pain in his eyes. They both deserve more than my indecision, but even amidst the storm of emotions, I recognize the truth of my own heart—I am not ready to choose, not yet. Maybe not ever. I need to work.

"Please," I add, my voice barely above a murmur. "Just stop."

And with those words, the tension doesn't dissipate but fractures into a myriad of complex emotions that fill the space between us, each shard reflecting the uncertainty of what is yet to come.

CHAPTER TWENTY TWO

The arena pulsates with the roar of the crowd, a living entity echoing the ferocity of the battle raging on the ice below. My gaze fixates on the players as they glide and clash, their movements a blur of precision and chaos. The Titans are locked in a merciless dance with the Crush, each check vibrating through the stands and into the core of every spectator.

Wes Carter is killing it out there. His jersey streaks across the rink like a comet. "Wild" is more than just a nickname; it's his mantra, his playing style carved into every forceful stride and brutal body check. The puck is an extension of him, obedient to his deft stickwork even amidst the frenzy.

But I can't help but keep my eyes on the bench, where Jamie is sitting, still as a statue. Despite the frenzy around him, his mouth is a straight, unreadable line.

He's dying to be out there. And it's not because of me.

My heart lurches, just as a collective gasp escapes the crowd as Wes slams another player into the boards, the sound of the reverberating impact disturbingly clear. A swift pass and the game carries on, but I'm left reeling from the violence of the collision. He's never played better—he's definitely kept his personal life off the ice.

Good for him.

From my vantage point at the edge of the rink, I've seen injuries that can end careers, witnessed the moment when dreams shatter on the ice. That's why I became a sports therapist: to save athletes from the fate that befell me. But it's not Wes I'm worried about tonight. He looks invincible, with his chaotic symphony of checks and shots. It's Jamie who is tearing relentlessly at my heartstrings.

With each passing second, my worry mounts until I'm more focused on Jamie than on the game. My fingers grip the railing until my knuckles turn white. There's a duty to my profession, a promise to guard the well-being of these athletes. Yet, as much as I try to remain detached, to view Jamie as just another player, the truth is undeniable: he isn't just anyone. He's Jamie—and I care so much about him.

Without warning, Jamie rises to his feet, hobbling toward the locker room with his head down. I look at the clock. Ten minutes to go, and the game is tied. Where is he headed?

I seize the moment of respite to rush down the corridor toward the locker room. The scent of sweat and determination meets me halfway, but it's Jamie's form that my eyes search for.

I find Jamie not in the locker room, but outside it, standing in the hallway, his head tilted back to the ceiling. My heart races—both from concern and something dangerously close to desire.

"Jamie," I start, my voice steady despite the turmoil within. "Are you okay?"

His eyes lock onto mine, a tumultuous ocean of blue, and there's a flash of something that looks like pain before he schools his features into indifference.

"What?" His tone is dismissive, almost defensive, but I'm not deterred.

"You looked upset out there," I say, gesturing vaguely toward the rink. "I know it must be so hard to not be on the ice. And…" I swallow hard, forcing the words out, "I just wanted to see if you were okay."

Jamie's stance stiffens, his jaw clenching tight enough to carve granite. A silence stretches between us, filled with the echoes of body checks and the crowd's roars.

Then he says, "That's not really your concern, is it?"

The words hit me like a slap to the face. I don't believe them.

"It is. I still care about you," I chide gently, though my heart thunders against my ribs. "What's going on, Jamie? I know it must be hard, watching Wes have the best game of his career while—"

He scoffs, raking a hand through his sandy hair. "You think this is about Wes?" There's a harsh laugh, void of humor. "No, Lara. This isn't about him. It's about you."

"Me?" I echo, taken aback.

"Yeah, you." The mask of the untamed player slips, revealing the raw edges beneath. "I can't help it. Every time I see him looking at you, talking to you, it drives me insane. I know I'm being irrational, but—" Jamie pauses, his gaze piercing through me, "it's your fault."

"My fault?" My voice cracks, incredulous.

"Because I've never felt this way before. Not about anyone." His confession hangs heavy in the air. "I'm losing my mind without you, and it's tearing me apart. You wanted space, I tried to give it to you, but it's like you're under my skin, and I can't get you out."

His vulnerability is palpable; it cloaks him more surely than any armor ever could. Here stands a man renowned for his courage on the ice, and he's brought low, because of me. I hate to see him like this when I can easily do something about it.

"Look, I know I'm a mess right now," he continues, each word laced with a desperate urgency. He drops his crutches and bridges the space between us with ease. "I know you want to concentrate on your work. But I don't know how to be around you and not want you. It's all or nothing with me, Lara. Always has been."

My heart hammers against my ribcage, echoing the intensity in his eyes. The world narrows down to this singular moment between heartbeats. And I, Lara Bennett, dedicated to healing and protecting, am left grappling with the reality of a man who doesn't want me just right now. He wants me forever.

Jamie's breath is hot against my skin, his gaze intense enough to sear through the ice that has formed around my heart. The air around us is thick with the scent of sweat and desperation, a heady mixture that seems to fuel the raw energy emanating from him. His hands, rough from years of handling a hockey stick, cradle my face with surprising gentleness. I'm caught in the dichotomy of Jamie—the fierce competitor on the ice and the man who now looks at me like I'm the only thing holding him together.

"I don't want to be on the ice if it means being without you. I'd give it all up in a second if I could have you," he whispers, voice ragged and full of an emotion I can't name. It's more than longing, deeper than desire. It's a plea wrapped in the echoes of a promise, one that sends shivers down my spine despite the warmth enveloping us.

His lips crash onto mine, a cascade of need and urgency that drowns out the roaring crowd. It's as if we're alone in this echoing cavern of noise, two souls colliding with the force of a body check. The kiss is nothing like our first sweet, tentative kiss. This is all-consuming, igniting fires that I've tried so hard to extinguish. His mouth moves against mine with a fervor that speaks of nights spent apart, of distance that only widened the chasm of our unspoken words.

I cling to him, my fingers digging into the fabric of his jersey, pulling him closer. Our breaths mingle, heavy and uneven, as if they're trying to merge into one. Time loses meaning when Jamie kisses me. There's only the here and now, the press of his body, the taste of his lips, the heartbeat that pounds in sync with mine.

“Choose me, Lara,” he says again as the kiss breaks, leaving us both gasping for air. “And you won’t be sorry.”

The buzzer signaling the end of the break pierces through the haze, a stark reminder of reality crashing back in. We separate, the space between us cold and unwelcome after the heat we shared. He leans down with grace to pick up his crutches, and I watch him move away, back toward the ice, leaving me to question everything.

CHAPTER TWENTY THREE

When the game ends, confetti rains down like a ticker tape parade, the cheers and whoops of victory echoing off the walls of the grand room. I stand amidst the sea of exuberance, my heart a fluttering bird trapped in a cage of uncertainty.

After the crowds funnel out, I find my way to the locker room, where the celebration is just beginning. Reporters are lined up, eager to get interviews with the star players, including Wes, the game's MVP. One look at the swarm in the corner, and I know he's likely at the center of it, right where he loves to be.

I stand on a bench to get a better look. It's just as I thought. Wes, ever the spectacle, is a whirlwind of charisma, absorbing the adulation with the ease of a man for whom winning is second nature. Across the room, his eyes find mine, a mischievous glint playing within their depths. He knows he's on top of the world, and in this moment, he wants to drag me up there with him.

"Listen up," Wes's voice booms, effortlessly cutting through the cacophony. The reporters huddle closer, recorders and cameras poised like hungry animals. "I've got something to say that's more important than any win."

He winks at me, and I feel the color drain from my face.

"I'm head over heels for this incredible woman right here!" He gestures grandiosely in my direction, his arm sweeping through the air as if presenting a grand prize. "Her name is Lara. Isn't she beautiful?"

All camera lenses swing my way. The room swells with collective gasps and murmurs, the reporters' excitement palpable. Wes eats it up, his smile wide and unapologetically theatrical. He basks in their attention, reveling in the spotlight that always seems to follow him. And there I am, caught in the glare, feeling more like a prop than a person in his showman's act.

I glare at him, frozen in horror as the reporters find me, asking my reaction. "No comment," I mutter, jumping from the bench and trying to make my way to the door.

But the reporters surround me. In the chaos, my gaze drifts and locks onto Jamie. He stands apart from the throng, his tall frame a pillar of stoic resolve. Those eyes of his are fixed on the scene before him, his expression stone-faced, unreadable. Jamie's presence is a silent beacon of sincerity among the revelry and pretense. I can tell he sees what's happening for what it is—a performance. Jamie has never needed the spotlight; he shines without trying.

Feeling a surge of panic, I pivot on my heel like a hockey player, avoiding an opponent. My name is called from all directions, but I dodge between bodies and flashbulbs, my only thought to escape. Somehow, I weave through the crowd, slipping out of the room like a ghost fleeing the light. My breath comes out in short bursts as I press myself against the wall just outside the door, listening to the muffled roar of the celebration I've left behind.

"Lara! Just a quick statement?" a persistent voice calls out, but I'm already moving, my legs carrying me away faster than my mind can process. I duck into a service hallway, the sound of my own footsteps a stark contrast to the jubilant chaos I've narrowly escaped. Through the twists and turns of the back corridors, I make my getaway, each step taking me further from the charade, closer to solitude.

I sneak away to my car in the lot. Alone at last, I let out a shaky sigh and close my eyes, willing my racing heart to calm. Wes's declaration, meant for the world, felt hollow to me. As I drive away, I can't help but wonder if genuine love can exist in the blinding glare of the public eye or if it flourishes better in the quiet corners where only sincere hearts dare to tread.

The key turns with a reluctant scrape inside the lock, and I shove my apartment door open. The familiar scent of lemon polish and the soft hum of the refrigerator are a stark contrast to the chaos I've left behind. Dropping my keys on the entryway table, I kick off my shoes and let my purse slide from my shoulder to the floor. It lands with a thud, the sound echoing in the stillness.

Then I run to the bedroom and change into my comfiest pj's. I need them right now.

I'm supposed to feel triumphant, the rush of victory flooding through me as it did for everyone else in that room, but all I feel is a deep, hollow emptiness. Wes's voice replays in my head, his words meant to be declarations of love sounding more like lines rehearsed for applause. My fingers trace the back of the couch as I walk past, each step heavier than the last until I collapse onto the cushions.

"Love" should not feel like this—like a performance staged for an audience, where the lights are too bright, and the smiles never reach the eyes. Wes never understood that. Or perhaps he understands it all too well and simply doesn't care. He's always been a showman, playing to the crowd, basking in their adulation. And just like that, I'm no different than any trophy he's ever won, displayed for the world to see, proof of his conquests.

A sigh escapes me, raw and ragged, as I grab my phone with a sense of resignation. Naomi's name is illuminated on the screen before I even realize I've dialed her number. She answers almost immediately, her voice a soothing balm to my frayed nerves.

"Hey, Lara," she says gently. "I saw the news. How are you holding up?"

"Ugh. Already?"

"Well…it was live, on the post-game show."

Great. Just what I need.

"Naomi," I start, my voice a mere whisper, "it was… it was all for show. Wes doesn't really care about me, not like I thought he did."

"Sweetie," she replies with a knowing tone, "Wes has always loved the spotlight. You know that. He thrives on it, lives for it, even. Maybe he does care for you, in his way, but Wes being Wes, he'll always share that love with the cameras first."

Her words, though spoken with compassion, slice through me because they echo the truth I've been trying to ignore. Wes might care for me, yes, but he loves the attention more. Always has, always will. And that's something I can't live with, not when my heart longs for a love that's quiet, steadfast, and just for me.

"Naomi, I'm done," I murmur into the phone, feeling the weight of the decision before me. "I can't be part of his spectacle anymore."

"Listen to your heart, Lara," she advises softly. "You deserve someone who loves you more than the fame, who values you beyond the wins and the spotlight. Someone who sees you, the real you."

Her words hang between us, heavy with unspoken truths and the gentle push toward a choice I've known I had to make but have been too afraid to face. Naomi has always been the one to help me see things clearly, to guide me back to myself when the world pulled me away.

"Thanks, Naomi," I say, a weary smile touching my lips. "I needed to hear that. I think I've always known, deep down. I just needed a friend to remind me."

"Always here for you," she affirms, and I can hear the smile in her voice. "Whatever you decide, I've got your back."

We talk a little longer, Naomi's steady presence a comforting anchor as I grapple with the turmoil inside me. When we finally say our goodbyes, I lean back against the sofa, breathing deeply, allowing her words to settle around me like a protective cloak. The choice is mine to make, and though I don't know what tomorrow will bring, I know I must choose a path true to my heart.

I stand at the window of my apartment, watching the city lights dance like distant stars fallen to earth. Naomi's words echo in my mind, a mantra that emboldens me, a tide pulling me toward a shore I've been avoiding for too long. The reflection staring back at me is one of resolve; the once uncertain gaze now holds a flicker of determination.

"Follow your heart," they say, as if it's the easiest thing in the world. But hearts are wild creatures, aren't they? Unpredictable and often leading us into territories unknown. Yet, there is a newfound clarity in the chaos of my feelings—a beacon amidst the storm, guiding me toward what feels authentic and true.

My heart knows its compass well. It understands the difference between the thrill of a chase and the quiet certainty of home. Memories flood through me: Wes with his electric smile, always keeping me on my toes, every moment a spectacle. But behind the fireworks, was there warmth? Was there solace?

Then there's Jamie—steady as the dawn, his laughter a melody that calms the restlessness in my soul. With him, life isn't a series of dazzling performances but a collection of genuine moments, each one precious because it's real.

I sit on the edge of my bed, elbows resting on knees, fingers laced together. The silence of the night envelops me like a comforting embrace, and in this stillness, my thoughts turn inward. I close my eyes and see myself not as the sprinter who chased after glory, but as the woman who yearns for something more enduring than fleeting fame. I've grown past the need for constant excitement; what I crave now is a connection that doesn't wane when the crowds disperse and the lights dim.

"Love is not a solo race," I whisper to the shadows, the words barely audible yet echoing around the empty room. My mind, so often cluttered with strategies and stats as a sports therapist, now ponders the matters of the heart. I've always known how to mend physical injuries, to restore strength and resilience. But repairing the fractures within my own heart? That's uncharted territory.

A memory surfaces, unbidden—Jamie's laughter, warm and genuine, like sunlight piercing through the overcast sky. It's a sound that untangles the knots in my chest, a soothing balm for the weariness that has seeped into my bones. I recall the times Jamie listened intently to my dreams and fears, never once dismissing them as trivial or outlandish. He offered solace without spectacle, companionship without conditions.

"Jamie…" His name is a revelation on my lips, a silent prayer that tastes of promise.

The realization blooms within me, steady and sure, like the first rays of dawn after the darkest night. I've been caught up in the allure of Wes's charisma, mistaking the rush of excitement for depth of feeling. But that's just it—it's an illusion, a fleeting sprint that leaves me breathless and alone at the finish line. With Jamie, it's different. It's real.

There's no grandstand, no roar of the crowd when I'm with him. Instead, there's a quiet understanding, a shared rhythm that needs no embellishment. I don't have to be the fastest or the strongest; I just have to be me. And isn't that what love should be? An acceptance of one's true self, an intertwining of souls that seek each other not for glory but for genuine connection?

In the solitude of my room, I allow myself to admit it—my heart belongs to Jamie. Not because he's the safer choice or because he fits some preconceived notion of the "right" partner. No, it's because with him, I find the courage to face my vulnerabilities, to cherish the moments that aren't measured by stopwatches or finish lines.

Love, I realize, isn't about the spectacle or the storybook endings. It's about finding someone who stands beside you, who sees your scars and doesn't flinch, who holds your dreams as tenderly as their own. It's about the slow build, the steady pace of two hearts learning to beat as one, not in a frenzied rush but in harmonious strides toward a shared future.

With every fiber of my being, I understand now what I need, what I want. It's not the blinding spotlight that comes with Wes's declarations. It's the gentle glow of Jamie's steadfast presence, the unwavering light that guides me home.

"Jamie," I say again, stronger this time, conviction lacing my voice. "It's always been you."

And in that admission, I find peace.

CHAPTER TWENTY FOUR

I text Wes, my fingers hovering over the send button for a moment longer than necessary. "Meet me at the old oak in Timberlake Park? We need to talk." The message feels too formal, too cold, but it's out there now, floating through the digital ether toward him.

Timberlake Park is a pocket of tranquility carved into the town's relentless pace, a place where the whispers of leaves and the soft gurgles of the stream are the only sounds that dare to break the hush. I chose it because it's far from the public eye, a secluded haven where the weight of the world seems lighter, where confessions don't echo quite as loudly.

When I arrive, the park greets me with open arms. The late-afternoon sun filters through the dense canopy, casting dappled shadows on the footpath. I love this time of day, the light waning, the air hushed yet expectant. Here, beneath the ancient oak that has borne witness to countless secrets and stolen kisses, I wait for Wes.

He strides into view, his athletic form unmistakable even from a distance. His casual confidence, the way his eyes scan the surroundings—it's clear he owns every space he enters. But here, in this quiet park, I see a different side of him. He's softer around the edges, less "Wild" Wes and more just... Wes.

"Hey," I say as he nears, the single word not encompassing all the nervous anticipation roiling inside of me.

"Hey, Lara," he replies, a smile tugging at his lips. "This is a nice spot. Private."

I nod, taking in his easy charm, the way his presence alone seems to fill the space between us. "I wanted somewhere we could talk without distractions."

"Sounds serious," he says, half-joking, running a hand through his hair—a habit I've come to associate with his rare moments of uncertainty.

I take a deep breath, steadying myself against the storm of emotions. "Wes, I've been doing a lot of thinking..."

"Never a good sign," he quips, but his smile fades as he sees the earnestness in my expression.

"Stop," I say with a small laugh, despite the gravity of the situation. "I want you to know how much I admire you. You're incredibly talented, Wes. On the ice, you move with such grace, such certainty—it's breathtaking. Your charm… it's not just bravado. There's genuine warmth there, a kindness that you don't let everyone see."

He cocks his head to the side, studying me, those perceptive eyes searching mine.

"Your dedication is inspiring," I continue. "The way you push through every challenge, turning setbacks into comebacks… It reminds me of… well, of the athlete I used to be. And the connection we share—our love for sports, our drive—it's something I never expected to find again, especially not with someone like you."

"Someone like me?" Wes asks, a playful note in his voice to mask the vulnerability I know is lurking just beneath the surface.

"Someone who challenges me," I clarify. "You make me want to be better, not just as a therapist but as a person. You've made an impact on my life, Wes, more than I thought possible in such a short time."

A silence settles between us, comfortable yet charged with unspoken words. The park, so serene and secluded, becomes our confessional, a sacred space where truths are laid bare and hearts are unraveled. Wes stands before me, the embodiment of everything I've just praised: strong yet gentle, fierce yet kind. And in this moment, I understand the true depth of our bond, one forged in admiration and mutual respect, even if it can't be what he wants it to be.

I draw in a breath, feeling the weight of the moment settle on my shoulders. The air is surprisingly cool for spring, carrying with it the faint scent of blossoming flowers from the nearby garden beds. I tuck a loose strand of hair behind my ear, buying myself a second before I face Wes. His gaze never wavers, and it's that intensity, the raw honesty in his eyes, that makes this all the harder.

"Wes," I start, my voice steadier than I feel, "I need to be honest with you about something important." I pause, searching for the right words, knowing there's no easy way to say this. "I wanted to be professional, but that didn't work. How could I be with you around? Then I thought I could just keep things casual, and that would be enough."

He shifts slightly, crossing his arms, but he doesn't interrupt. His silence is permission to continue, and I take it like a lifeline tossed in turbulent seas.

"Somewhere along the line," I say, swallowing down the lump forming in my throat, "my feelings got complicated. Not for us, not for what we have, but..." My heart hammers against my chest as I admit the truth that's been eating at me. "But for Jamie. I'm in love with him."

The confession hangs in the air between us, and I watch as Wes's expression flickers—surprise etching his features, followed by an unmistakable shadow of disappointment. He looks away for a moment, his jaw clenching, and I see the struggle as he processes my words. This vulnerability in "Wild" Wes Carter, the bad boy who seemed untouchable, reveals the depth of his feelings and the hope he must have harbored.

After a heartbeat, he turns back to me, his eyes meeting mine with a clarity that's piercing. "Lara," he begins, his voice rough around the edges, "I'd be lying if I said I hadn't hoped for... more. You're incredible, you know? And yeah, I wanted you."

My chest tightens at the raw honesty in his words, the admission of his own feelings that he lays out with such bravery. It's a side of Wes few people get to see—the openness, the willingness to be vulnerable even when it hurts.

"Thank you," I whisper, my gratitude for his understanding mixing with a pang of regret that I have to cause him any pain. "You mean a lot to me, Wes, truly. I hope you know that our friendship—it's something I treasure. And I hope we can still support each other, no matter what."

There's a long pause where we simply look at each other, the connection we share pulsing like a living thing. Then, slowly, Wes nods. "We're good, Lara," he assures me, although I can see the effort it takes for him to smile. "Always."

With those words, a sense of closure wraps around us, bittersweet and yet necessary. We part ways then, each step I take away from him laced with the complex emotions of what we've shared and what might have been.

As I walk toward the practice facility, my mind races ahead to Jamie, to the future that awaits us. There's a flutter of anticipation in my belly, a spark of hope that maybe, just maybe, everything will fall into place.

The door to the practice facility swings open with a familiar creak, the sound now laden with a significance I can't quite shake. My heart hammers against my ribcage, a steady reminder of the choice that's brought me here. The scent of sweat and determination fills the air, mingling with the faint clang of metal as I step inside. There he is—Jamie, a study in focus, lifting weights at the bench press in a rhythm that mirrors the pulse racing through my veins.

"Need a spot?" I offer, my voice steadier than I feel.

He pauses mid-lift, the bar hovering above him as his eyes lock onto mine. There's a hesitancy there, a guardedness that I've put in place, and it twists something inside me. He sets the weights back on the rack with a clank and sits up, wiping his brow with the back of his hand.

"Since when do you show up unannounced?" His tone is light, but I sense the wariness beneath it.

"Since today," I say, taking a step closer to him. I'm suddenly aware of the space between us, charged with all the words we've left unsaid. "Jamie, I owe you an apology. I've been… I've made things complicated, and I'm sorry if I drove you crazy."

I watch the lines around his eyes soften, the beginning of understanding dawning there. My fingers tremble slightly as I gather the strands of my resolve, clutching them tightly before they can slip away.

"Thank you, Jamie. Thank you for being patient, for being there—even when I didn't know I needed someone. You've been a constant in the chaos, and I…" A breath shudders out of me, my next words the most terrifying and liberating I've ever spoken. "I've made a decision. It's you, Jamie. I choose you."

His reaction is still for a moment, eyes searching mine for any hint of doubt. But there's none to be found, only the clarity and certainty that have eluded me until now. Slowly, a smile begins to curve his lips, the joy in his expression blossoming like the first rays of dawn piercing through the darkness.

"Really?" he asks, his voice a mix of hope and disbelief.

"Really," I affirm, with a nod that feels like the first step into a new beginning.

Despite the cast, in one fluid motion, Jamie rises to his feet and closes the distance between us. His arms encircle me in an embrace that speaks of relief and homecoming. And then his lips are on mine, a kiss that seals promises and whispers futures. It's a kiss that writes the end of one story and the beginning of another.

"We don't have to tell anyone," he murmurs against my lips, his breath warm and tinged with the remnants of exertion. "If it's going to rattle Lawson. We can keep this between us, if that's what you want."

But secrecy feels like a backward step, a retreat into shadows we no longer need to hide within. I draw back just enough to meet his gaze, my own shining with a conviction that feels unbreakable.

"No," I say, my voice filled with a newfound strength. "I don't mind if the world knows. In fact, I want them to."

He raises an eyebrow. "And Coach Lawson?"

I smile. "If she fires me for following my heart, then fine. I want you more than I want this job."

Jamie's grin widens, reflecting the leap my heart takes at the thought of facing tomorrow and every day after with him by my side. The weight of uncertainty lifts, leaving behind the lightness of a path chosen, a love declared. Here, in this temple of physical endurance, we find the start of our emotional journey—one where I am no longer running from my feelings but racing headlong into them, with Jamie at my side.

I step back from Jamie, the flush of his elation still warming the air between us. My heart is a drumline, pounding in time with the thrum of life all around—the distant clank of weights, the muffled echoes of sneakers on the gym floor, the steady breaths that lift Jamie's chest. I watch him, this man who has become my anchor in a tumultuous sea, and I know that this moment is a turning point.

"Let's go grab some dinner," I say, the words bubbling up from a place of lightness within me. "My treat."

He chuckles, wiping the sweat from his brow with the back of his hand. It leaves a streak across his forehead, a badge of his dedication to everything he does, including waiting for me. "You sure? You don't have to—"

"Jamie," I interrupt, my voice firm yet playful, "it's not up for discussion. You've earned it, after the hell I put you through."

The gym around us fades into the background as we lock eyes, and there's a silent understanding that passes between us. He nods, a small smile playing on his lips, and I can see the shift in him—the easing of tension that had coiled tight in his shoulders for too long.

We exit the practice facility together, the setting sun casting long shadows across the parking lot. The colors of dusk paint the sky in hues of deep purple and fiery orange, a beautiful end to a day that's been nothing short of transformative. As we reach our cars, parked side by side, Jamie's hand finds mine, his fingers intertwining with mine in a perfect fit.

"Hey, Lara?"

"Yeah?" I turn toward him, our connected hands swinging slightly between us.

"What if I'm not wild enough for you?" His voice is earnest, his blue eyes darkening with emotion.

"I don't need wild," I reply, squeezing his hand. "I just need you. Exactly as you are."

We stand there, a comfortable silence enveloping us like a shared blanket. This is what certainty feels like—an unshakable foundation built on mutual respect and affection.

Then he says, "Can we have tacos?"

I giggle. I think he just read my mind. "Tacos it is!"

As we drive off in Jamie's car to find a quiet spot for dinner, my mind races ahead. There will be questions from the team, from friends who've watched the drama unfold, from Wes. There will be challenges as we navigate this new terrain together. But for now, those concerns are distant whispers drowned out by the promise of the present.

I glance over at Jamie, his profile illuminated by the dashboard lights, and feel a surge of anticipation for what's to come. We're embarking on a journey neither of us expected but one we're both ready to embrace wholeheartedly. And as the first chapter of our story closes, I'm eager to turn the page, to begin writing the next with Jamie by my side, our lives intertwined like the threads of a tapestry we'll weave together—one of love, friendship, and endless possibilities.

CHAPTER TWENTY FIVE

The sun dips low on the horizon, casting a golden glow over the beach where our team celebrates. The sound of waves crashing against the shore blends with the laughter and cheers of the players who've just secured their spot in the playoffs. I stand at the edge of it all, letting the cool breeze ruffle my hair, now loose and free from its usual ponytail confinement.

"Hey, Bennett!" someone calls out, and a Frisbee whizzes by, beckoning me to join the game. I smile, declining with a wave. My heart swells seeing them so happy, knowing I played a part in getting us here. After months of pushing boundaries and challenging old-school methods, we've found a rhythm, my newfangled techniques weaving into the fabric of the team's regimen.

"Can I have a moment?" A voice, serious and firm, cuts through my reverie. Coach Lawson stands before me, her face unreadable. Tension coils in my stomach as I nod, excusing myself from the festivities. We step away from the crowd, her tall figure casting a long shadow on the sand. The team's joyous shouts become a distant hum as Pat's gaze locks onto mine, those steely eyes that once scrutinized my every move now softening.

"Coach Lawson?" I prompt, fighting to keep my voice steady.

"Look, Lara," she begins, her voice uncharacteristically gentle, "I've been around this game a long time. Seen hotshots come and go, thinking they can change the way things are done." She pauses, looking out toward the setting sun. "But you… you're different."

I blink in surprise, unsure where this is going.

"Your methods, your ideas about therapy and recovery—I was wrong to dismiss them so quickly." Pat's confession hangs between us, sincere and heavy. "You've brought something to this team that I didn't even know we needed. And for that, I owe you an apology."

My breath catches at her words. This admission from a woman who's built her career on grit and traditionalism is more than just recognition; it's validation.

"Thank you, Coach," I reply, feeling a weight lift off my shoulders. "I just want what's best for the team."

She nods, a rare smile tugging at the corners of her mouth. "And you've given them that. You've proven yourself invaluable, Lara." Her gaze returns to mine, filled with newfound respect. "I should've seen it sooner."

"Better late than never," I say with a small laugh, and for a brief moment, the barrier between coach and sports therapist crumbles, leaving just two professionals who share a love for the game.

Pat takes a deep breath and shifts her stance, the sand beneath our feet giving way slightly under the pressure. "I know about you and Jamie," she starts, and my heart skips a beat, bracing for the backlash I've feared since the start of our not-so-secret romance.

"Yes…we were going to tell you about—"

"Look, I'm not one to recommend personal relationships within the team," Pat continues, her voice surprisingly calm, even reflective. "But I can't deny it either—Jamie's never played better." She glances over my shoulder, presumably at where Jamie is celebrating with his teammates, laughter and playful shouts reaching us as gentle waves lap the shore. "You got him out on the ice for the last regular season game. We honestly thought he wasn't going to be here for playoffs. So that's all you."

"He's an excellent player," I manage to say, trying to gauge where this conversation is leading. "And he was very committed to his rehabilitation. He's a therapist's dream."

"Indeed," she agrees. "And he seems… different, happier. He cares about you, Lara. It's as clear as day." A rare vulnerability flashes in Pat's eyes, like she's allowing herself to see beyond the game plans and strategies to the humans playing them.

"Thank you," I whisper, touched by her perceptiveness and acceptance. And then she hits me with the unexpected.

"I want to sign you to the Titans for a five-year contract." Her words tumble out, almost eager. "Your work here… it's just beginning."

The news sweeps over me like a tidal wave. Five years. Five more seasons of doing what I love, with the possibility of changing more lives, shaping careers, and maybe even the future of the sport—all while being close to Jamie. Excitement bubbles up inside me, and I struggle to keep my composure.

"Five years?" I echo, my voice a mixture of shock and elation.

“Five years,” she confirms, a grin breaking through her usual stern demeanor. “If you’ll have us.”

“Of course I’ll have you!” The words escape before I can think, and my professional decorum slips into a joyous laugh. In my excitement, I throw my arms around her, hugging her. It takes a moment, but she hugs back.

“Good,” Pat says, clapping me on the back before turning away, leaving me to bask in the glow of the offer and the setting sun.

***

As the sun melts orange on the horizon, I scan the celebration, seeking out the one face that has come to mean so much to me in recent weeks. The players are a blur of jerseys and smiles until finally, my gaze locks onto Jamie. Our eyes meet across the distance, and the noise around us seems to hush. His expression softens, a silent question passing between us as I navigate through the throng of bodies toward him.

“Hey,” I say, my voice barely above a whisper when I reach him. The simple greeting carries the weight of everything unsaid, every stolen moment we’ve shared.

“Hey yourself,” he replies, his eyes searching mine. There’s a hint of wonder, a touch of hope mirrored in his look that sends shivers down my spine.

“Can we talk? Somewhere… private?” My question hangs in the air, charged with anticipation.

“Lead the way,” Jamie says, intuiting the seriousness from the tone of my voice.

We slip away from the crowd, moving to where the beach gives way to a grassy dune topped with swaying sea oats. Away from the prying eyes and raucous cheers, I turn to face him, taking in his hair tousled by the ocean breeze, the stubble accentuating his jawline. He waits, patient and steady as ever, for me to speak. My pulse races, knowing that what comes next could change everything.

The bright stars flicker above us like a promise, and the gentle murmur of waves against the shore underscores the stillness in my heart. Jamie stands before me, the soft glow of moonlight casting his features into a tapestry of light and shadow. I take a deep breath, feeling the gravity of my own emotions as they threaten to spill over.

"Jamie," I begin, my voice carrying the tremble of my racing pulse. "These past weeks have been… unexpected. You've shown me kindness, strength, and a patience I never knew existed." I pause, searching his eyes for understanding. "I came here to heal others, but somewhere along the way, you've started to heal something in me."

His gaze holds mine, unwavering, encouraging me to continue.

"And I'm so happy we're together. And will be together, if you'll have me."

He tilts his head, understanding dawning. "Wait. Are you saying…?"

"She offered me a five-year contract," I say, clapping my hands together in excitement.

"Yes!" He pulls me into a hug. "Of course I'll have you. You're moving in with me."

We'd talked about the future, but it was hard without knowing where I would be next season. We knew I'd have to go where work took me. But our best-case scenario was Pat extending my contract, because it meant I could move into Jamie's house overlooking the coast. And now, it's actually happening.

A sigh escapes me, releasing the tension that's been building inside as Jamie nestles his face into my hair. "I love you so much, Jamie. I never planned for this, never imagined I could find someone who understands me the way you do. You're not just the perfect boyfriend; you're the perfect partner. And I'm so grateful for you."

For a moment, Jamie doesn't speak. Then he pulls away. His hand reaches up, gently brushing a stray lock of my hair off my cheek, and I can see the resolve in his eyes—clear and profound.

"Lara," he says, his voice low and steady, "there was a time when I thought discipline and dedication were all I needed to be complete. But you've taught me that there's more to life—more to me. You've become my compass, my unexpected north star, guiding me to a happiness I didn't know was possible."

He cups my face in his hands, thumbs caressing my cheeks with tenderness. "I love you too, more than I ever thought I could love anyone. I don't just want to be your perfect boyfriend or partner. I want to be your everything. And no matter what happens, no matter where life takes us, I promise I'll never let you go."

His declaration wraps around me like a blanket, solid and true. In his eyes, I see our future unfolding, an uncharted territory we're ready to explore together. The fear of the unknown no longer seems daunting because, with Jamie, every uncertainty feels like an opportunity for discovery.

The world seems to slow, the revelry of our teammates fading into a distant murmur. Jamie's hands still cradle my face with a gentleness that sends shivers down my spine. His eyes search mine, holding me captive in their oceanic depths. I can taste the salt in the air, feel the soft sand give way under my feet, each grain a silent witness to the precipice we find ourselves on.

"Jamie," I whisper, my breath hitching as his gaze drops to my lips. The anticipation coils tighter within me, every nerve ending alight with the knowledge of what's to come. I watch, mesmerized, as his eyelids flutter closed, an unspoken invitation that pulls me into his orbit.

My heart thunders against my ribs, a drumbeat syncing with the ebb and flow of the waves behind us. It feels like the first time I took off from the starting blocks, the adrenaline, the focus, the rush—all converging in this single moment. My hands rise, trembling slightly, to rest on his chest. I can feel the solid beat of his heart, a mirror of my own.

Suddenly, our lips meet, and it's as though fireworks explode in the distance, their brilliant colors painting the night sky just for us. Jamie kisses me with a passion that is both a question and an answer, a dance of give and take that speaks more than words ever could. I respond in kind, pouring all the emotions I've held back into this one kiss, sealing the promises we've made to each other.

His arms wrap around me, pulling me closer until there's no space left between us. The kiss deepens, tender yet fervent, as if we're both trying to memorize the feel of each other. I lose myself in the sensation, in the taste of him, the sound of our mingled breaths, the warmth of his skin. This isn't just a kiss; it's a declaration, an acknowledgment of the journey we've endured to reach this point—together.

As we finally break apart, gasping for air, a sense of peace settles over me. Jamie's forehead rests against mine, his breath warm on my face. We're both smiling, and there's a lightness in my chest—an effervescent joy that bubbles out of me as a laugh. He chuckles too, the sound resonating deep in his chest.

"Ready to face whatever comes next?" he asks, his voice laced with hope and an unwavering confidence that buoys my spirits.

"Absolutely," I reply, my determination matching his. With Jamie by my side, the future isn't something to fear but something to embrace with open arms.

We stand there, locked in an embrace, the stars above us and the sea at our backs. The chapter of uncertainties closes, and a new one begins—a chapter filled with contentment, with love, and a shared readiness to take on the world. Together, we watch the horizon, where the dark sea meets the night sky, knowing that whatever challenges lie ahead, we'll face them as one.

NOW AVAILABLE!

MELTING THE ICE
(A Timberlake Titans Hockey Romance —Book 3)

In the town of Timberlake, hockey is more than just a sport; it's a way of life, and semi-pro team the Titans are local heroes. When ice choreographer Lila Mercer is assigned to work closely with the Titans to improve their skating performance, she falls hard—not on the ice, but for two of the players. Who will she choose between team captain Nathan and notorious enforcer Alex?

A riveting new sports romance series by Fiona Grace, #1 bestselling author of Murder in the Manor, which has over 10,000 five-star reviews!

MELTING THE ICE (A TIMBERLAKE TITANS HOCKEY ROMANCE) is the third book in the series, which begins with RINKSIDE ROMANCE (Book #1).

Dive into the world of the Timberlake Titans, where a blend of athletics and amorous escapades awaits, transporting you to a charming locale filled with clever humor, tender interludes, and surprising turns. Get ready to fall for entrancing new lead characters who are poised to steal your heart.

Future books in the series are also available!

"Very entertaining. I highly recommend this book to the permanent library of any reader that appreciates a very well written mystery, with some twists and an intelligent plot. You will not be disappointed. Excellent way to spend a cold weekend!"
--Books and Movie Reviews, Roberto Mattos (regarding Murder in the Manor)

"The story line wasn't just a who done it, but had a story about her life and romance, including village life. Very entertaining."
--Amazon reviewer (regarding Murder in the Manor)

"It has endearing and sometimes quirky characters, a plot that keeps you reading and the right amount of romance. I can't wait to start book two!"
--Amazon reviewer (regarding Murder in the Manor)

"What a great story of murder, romance, new beginnings, love, friend ships and a wonderful cascade of mystery."
--Amazon reviewer (regarding Murder in the Manor)

"This is a clean contemporary romance that you will find hard to put down!"
--Amazon reviewer (regarding Always, Forever)

"A bit of romance and a very determined woman! I have read many of Fiona Grace's novels and loved every one of them—this was no exception. I am looking forward to reading the rest of this new series!"
--Amazon reviewer (regarding Always, With You)

Fiona Grace

Fiona Grace is author of the LACEY DOYLE COZY MYSTERY series, comprising nine books; of the TUSCAN VINEYARD COZY MYSTERY series, comprising seven books; of the DUBIOUS WITCH COZY MYSTERY series, comprising three books; of the BEACHFRONT BAKERY COZY MYSTERY series, comprising six books; of the CATS AND DOGS COZY MYSTERY series, comprising nine books; of the ELIZA MONTAGU COZY MYSTERY series, comprising nine books (and counting); of the ENDLESS HARBOR ROMANTIC COMEDY series, comprising nine books (and counting); of the INN AT DUNE ISLAND ROMANTIC COMEDY series, comprising seven books (and counting); of the INN BY THE SEA ROMANTIC COMEDY series, comprising five books (and counting); of the ALICE BLOOM COZY MYSTERY series, comprising five (and counting); of the MAID AND THE MANSION COZY MYSTERY series, comprising five books (and counting); of the MAGNOLIA BAY COZY MYSTERY series, comprising five books (and counting); and of the TIMBERLAKE TITANS HOCKEY ROMANCE series, comprising five books (and counting).

Fiona would love to hear from you, so please visit www.fionagraceauthor.com to receive free ebooks, hear the latest news, and stay in touch.

BOOKS BY FIONA GRACE

MAGNOLIA BAY COZY MYSTERY
THE TAINTED TAFFY (Book #1)
A MASKED MURDER (Book #2)
A CAFE CONFESSION (Book #3)
THE FROZEN FIND (Book #4)
A CURIOUS CURSE (Book #5)

TIMBERLAKE TITANS HOCKEY ROMANCE
RINKSIDE ROMANCE (Book #1)
FLIRTY FACEOFF (Book #2)
MELTING THE ICE (Book #3)
THE PUCK STOPS HERE (Book #4)
GLOVES DROP, LOVE BLOOMS (Book #5)

ALICE BLOOM COZY MYSTERY
MURDER IN THE MARIGOLDS (Book #1)
RUIN IN THE ROSES (Book #2)
DECEIT IN THE DAFFODILS (Book #3)
SCANDAL IN THE SAFFRON (Book #4)
CATASTROPHE IN THE CARNATIONS (Book #5)

THE MAID AND THE MANSION COZY MYSTERY
A MYSTERIOUS MURDER (Book #1)
A SCANDALOUS DEATH (Book #2)
A MISSING GUEST (Book #3)
AN UNSOLVABLE CRIME (Book #4)
AN IMPOSSIBLE HEIST (Book #5)

INN BY THE SEA ROMANTIC COMEDY
A NEW LOVE (Book #1)
A NEW CHANCE (Book #2)
A NEW HOME (Book #3)
A NEW LIFE (Book #4)
A NEW ME (Book #5)

THE INN AT DUNE ISLAND ROMANTIC COMEDY

A CHANCE LOVE (Book #1)
A CHANCE FALL (Book #2)
A CHANCE ROMANCE (Book #3)
A CHANCE CHRISTMAS (Book #4)
A CHANCE ENGAGEMENT (Book #5)
A CHANCE DREAM (Book #6)
A CHANCE WEDDING (Book #7)

ENDLESS HARBOR ROMANTIC COMEDY

ALWAYS, WITH YOU (Book #1)
ALWAYS, FOREVER (Book #2)
ALWAYS, PLUS ONE (Book #3)
ALWAYS, TOGETHER (Book #4)
ALWAYS, LIKE THIS (Book #5)
ALWAYS, FATED (Book #6)
ALWAYS, FOR LOVE (Book #7)
ALWAYS, JUST US (Book #8)
ALWAYS, IN LOVE (Book #9)

ELIZA MONTAGU COZY MYSTERY

MURDER AT THE HEDGEROW (Book #1)
A DALLOP OF DEATH (Book #2)
CALAMITY AT THE BALL (Book #3)
A SPEAKEASY DEMISE (Book #4)
A FLAPPER FATALITY (Book #5)
BUMPED BY A DAME (Book #6)
A DOLL'S DEBACLE (Book #7)
A FELLA'S RUIN (Book #8)
A GAL'S OFFING (Book #9)

LACEY DOYLE COZY MYSTERY

MURDER IN THE MANOR (Book#1)
DEATH AND A DOG (Book #2)
CRIME IN THE CAFE (Book #3)
VEXED ON A VISIT (Book #4)
KILLED WITH A KISS (Book #5)
PERISHED BY A PAINTING (Book #6)
SILENCED BY A SPELL (Book #7)
FRAMED BY A FORGERY (Book #8)

CATASTROPHE IN A CLOISTER (Book #9)

TUSCAN VINEYARD COZY MYSTERY

AGED FOR MURDER (Book #1)
AGED FOR DEATH (Book #2)
AGED FOR MAYHEM (Book #3)
AGED FOR SEDUCTION (Book #4)
AGED FOR VENGEANCE (Book #5)
AGED FOR ACRIMONY (Book #6)
AGED FOR MALICE (Book #7)

DUBIOUS WITCH COZY MYSTERY

SKEPTIC IN SALEM: AN EPISODE OF MURDER (Book #1)
SKEPTIC IN SALEM: AN EPISODE OF CRIME (Book #2)
SKEPTIC IN SALEM: AN EPISODE OF DEATH (Book #3)

BEACHFRONT BAKERY COZY MYSTERY

BEACHFRONT BAKERY: A KILLER CUPCAKE (Book #1)
BEACHFRONT BAKERY: A MURDEROUS MACARON (Book #2)
BEACHFRONT BAKERY: A PERILOUS CAKE POP (Book #3)
BEACHFRONT BAKERY: A DEADLY DANISH (Book #4)
BEACHFRONT BAKERY: A TREACHEROUS TART (Book #5)
BEACHFRONT BAKERY: A CALAMITOUS COOKIE (Book #6)

CATS AND DOGS COZY MYSTERY

A VILLA IN SICILY: OLIVE OIL AND MURDER (Book #1)
A VILLA IN SICILY: FIGS AND A CADAVER (Book #2)
A VILLA IN SICILY: VINO AND DEATH (Book #3)
A VILLA IN SICILY: CAPERS AND CALAMITY (Book #4)
A VILLA IN SICILY: ORANGE GROVES AND VENGEANCE (Book #5)
A VILLA IN SICILY: CANNOLI AND A CASUALTY (Book #6)

Printed in Great Britain
by Amazon

43786780R00088